KNOWING THE OGRE'S HEART

A TROLLKIN LOVERS NOVEL

LYONNE RILEY

INTRODUCTION

After the death of his parents at the hands of human villagers, Cragnorr was orphaned—until Mia, only a girl herself, rescued him. She's kept him a secret all his life, and the silent, gentle Cragnorr has made it his mission to protect Mia.

But when Cragnorr's presence is discovered by the village, the two of them must run. While Cragnorr and Mia try to survive in the wilderness, their bond of friendship evolves into something else... until they're taken prisoner by bandits.

Cragnorr is forced to fight in the bandits' gladiator pit, while Mia watches from the bandit king's side. Can they escape this terrible place? Or will the peaceful giant finally unleash the vicious monster he keeps hidden inside?

CONTENT WARNINGS

Contains spoilers.

- Graphic depictions of sex
- Size difference

- Stretching and stuffing
- Breeding kink
- Murdered parents
- Physical abuse
- Mistreatment and neglect
- Captivity
- Gore
- Fighting pits and gladiator fights
- On-page death
- Compelled breeding in captivity
- Public torture/lashing
- Threat of sexual violence
- Gambling
- Alcoholism
- Pregnancy
- Birth

To my ogre

CHAPTER 1

MIA

It's a difficult journey to get up the cliffs to the cave where Cragnorr lives, but I've gotten quite good at it over the years. He doesn't need me to bring food to him as often now, as he takes care of most of his own needs by hunting and foraging, but I always make sure to save some bread, cheese, and smoked meat for him when I can. He loves cured salami the most.

Yesterday, I got some sweets from the traveling merchant that came through town, and I thought Cragnorr would like them. They're in my bag as I head up the mountainside.

My parents don't bother asking anymore where I'm going when I leave. Mom is always busy at her loom, making rugs and blankets to sell at the market. Dad has a jewelry shop in town where he repairs earrings and watches and sometimes makes rings. As long as I'm not getting into trouble, which I never have, they don't care how or where I spend my day. They haven't pressured me yet into finding my own trade, hoping secretly that a man will come along and offer to marry me. Then they can send me on my way with a clear conscience.

But I would never marry someone, not if it meant I had to leave Cragnorr.

I was ten when the village hunters went out in a party, searching for the cougar that was plucking off our livestock. Instead of a cougar in the woods, the hunters found a pair of ogres—creatures we thought had long disappeared.

The hunters returned with their swords smeared in blood, and told everyone in town that the ogres put up a fight before they were felled like ancient trees. The hunting party all seemed so proud of themselves for butchering a family.

Trollkin are our natural enemies, of course. We have been at war with the trolls and orcs for as long as anyone can remember, and unfortunately for Cragnorr's parents, ogres are lumped in with them. I had never seen a trollkin with my own eyes before, so that night, my curiosity got the better of me and I went out to look. They must be terrifying to stir such fear in the villagers.

I followed the trail left behind by the horses' hoof prints deep into the woods, and there I found two bodies, both enormous. One ogre and one ogress, eyes open and unseeing, bodies covered in their own blood. Empty packs lay beside them, clearly pillaged by the hunters.

The ogres were not nearly as monstrous as I'd been led to believe. Their tusks were large, yes—but they wore simple clothes that looked handmade, and their packs were similarly woven. Their faces were soft, quiet, almost peaceful despite the blood.

What had they done to deserve this besides live?

That was when I heard something shifting up in the branches of a tree. I wondered if I'd made a mistake coming out here, and the threat still lingered. But at ten years old, my curiosity was powerful —more powerful than my fear of the unknown, so I climbed into the tree to get a better look at whatever was hiding there.

It's been fourteen years now since I found a little ogre clinging to a tree trunk, tears falling from his eyes in perfect silence. That's always how he's been: besides a word here and there, he barely makes a sound. But I don't blame him, having seen what he did.

The tears on Cragnorr's face glistened in the moonlight. He was so young and so helpless, I was surprised at how big he was. Perhaps I should have been frightened of him, but all I saw was a lost child who had no one left.

"Give me your hand," I told him, and when at last he took my open palm in his, we hopped down from the tree together.

This small ogre didn't want to let me go after that, but I couldn't take him home or the villagers would simply kill him like they did his parents. So I pledged to hide him and protect him, knowing I could never fix what my kind had done, but hoping I could keep him safe until he was old enough to fend for himself.

I don't know how old Cragnorr was when I found him, but it seems to me that ogres grow similar to the way humans do, so I would say he was six or seven. I led him to an old, abandoned shed, where I brought him blankets and a lamp and whatever food I could scrounge up that wouldn't be noticed. Often, I gave him my own dinner so no one would ask questions, and eventually, he became comfortable enough that he told me his name.

Cragnorr. That's one of the few words he's ever said. I don't know if he's always been quiet, or if watching his parents murdered in front of him killed the words in his throat.

Cragnorr lived the first few years of his life in that shed, trying to stay a secret from my parents. I visited him whenever possible, until one day my father talked about using the old shed again to store parts, and we had to come up with a different solution. Cragnorr was getting much bigger, anyway, and he needed a home that could accommodate him.

After weeks of searching, he finally found a cave that was livable. He was drawn to it in the way I think ogres are, and with my help, he was able to live there alone. He really should have been with his mother, or other ogres like him, but I was all he had. I wonder how many remain, or if Cragnorr and his family are the last. He could have left long ago, but instead he's chosen to stay, living up on the mountain that overshadows our village.

I navigate the switchbacks that lead up the cliff until I reach the ledge, where I can find his cave. The lamp inside is burning, casting a bright yellow glow from the low archway. I follow it inside, and as I enter, Cragnorr gets up out of one of the two chairs he built out of logs and scrap wood. When we were younger and he was smaller, I would run over and hug him whenever I came to visit, but then we both grew up in different ways. Sometimes I still want to throw my arms around him, but it would feel inappropriate.

"I brought you something," I sing-song, sitting at the little table Cragnorr built. Over the years his cave has become a home, and I've brought him what supplies I can to build with. I pour out my backpack over the table, candies spilling everywhere. Cragnorr's amber eyes get big.

"Sweets," I tell him happily. "Remember the last time I brought some and you really liked the caramel? I made sure to get lots of those this time."

Cragnorr reaches out with one massive, grey-green hand and swipes one of the tiny candies I've brought. When the candy is exposed to him, gleaming in the lamplight, he plops it into his mouth.

"It's so good, right?" I ask. "I thought you would like those." In answer, Cragnorr lets out a happy noise. "Now don't eat all of them at once, like you did that one time. Remember how sick you got? I don't know the next time that merchant will be back."

Cragnorr thoughtfully sucks on the candy in his mouth. It's nice to be with him again, surrounded by his calm, collected energy.

"I spent some time with Dad working on his latest project," I tell him. "He's making some wedding rings for a couple in town, and he's teaching me how to set the jewels."

Cragnorr nods along while he eats.

"I'm getting a lot better at it. Next we're going to do some engraving!" I love working with my hands. "Maybe I can make you something?"

He smiles, then holds out one hand like he's imagining a ring around one of his big fingers.

"But I don't think we have a gauge big enough..." I trail off. I don't mean to remind him again that he doesn't fit in the human world, but he doesn't seem to mind.

It's only when my head starts to get a little fuzzy, and the world tilts around me, that I realize it's getting late and I should start back home.

Cragnorr's brows tilt down and his lips curve into a frown, the same as always when it comes time for me to go. He tries to hide how sad it makes him to watch me leave, but it's there anyway, underneath the surface.

I've encouraged Cragnorr to go explore before, suggesting that he look for others of his kind and find a place where he might truly belong. As awful as it would feel to lose him, it would be what's best for him.

But every time I bring it up, Cragnorr shakes his head as if this is an impossibility.

When I finally say, "I've got to get to bed," he rises up to his full height, dense and thick with muscle, and follows me out of the cave. I'm not sure how he became so strong, but I get the sense that I don't know most of the things he does during the day when I'm not around.

Cragnorr holds up the lamp while I work my way down the cliffside. I've gotten good at this, but I know better than to become cocky and possibly fall. His lamp guides my way until he's out of sight.

Cragnorr

I hate watching her go. I always have, and I always will.

Mia is joy and light. When she comes it is summer, and when she leaves it is winter again. I love listening to her musical voice, the way she spins the story of how she spent her day, making it sound mystical and magical.

I've grown used to watching her leave me, though. I know that she'll be back the next day, or the day after. Maybe our visits are different now than they used to be, but I will see her again.

When we were young, she would take me to bathe at the lake, and always led me along by the hand. We'd soap ourselves, and then Mia would rinse her sun-kissed brown skin before rinsing mine. Now my little human keeps a polite distance, only occasionally touching me when her small fingers land on mine as we reach for the same piece of fruit.

I miss when Mia wasn't afraid of me. When she found me, we were nearly the same size. The change happened when I grew taller, and taller, and my body filled out even thicker and firmer until I was towering over her. That's when she stopped putting her arms around me, and I miss the scent of her lavender-scented soap. I think about it long after she leaves, and I wonder what it would feel like to hold her again now that she's all soft curves.

Perhaps this is why we don't hug anymore.

Sometimes I wish I could follow her home to make sure she gets back safely, but she's forbidden me from coming too close to the village. I still remember the human men who put their bullets and swords through my parents that fateful day, and I know she fears that would be my dead body if they ever found me living here.

So I do what she asks and remain in my cave, only leaving to find food or supplies in the woods. I will always do what my Mia asks of me.

Like I do every night, I close up the cave with a wooden plank that fits neatly into the entrance, then make my way into the back, where the walls and ceiling draw in closer and tighter. Here I lie down on my pile of furs and pelts, wishing I could tell Mia that I won't harm her just because I'm so big now. That I would *never* harm her.

This is why I refuse to leave her to look for other ogres who may or may not exist. It's my job to protect her. I live on this mountain overlooking the village so I can always keep an eye out, so I'm prepared should danger ever come. She saved me, and so until I die, I will watch over her.

After extinguishing the lamp, I lie down in my bed and stare up into the darkness for what feels like hours, remembering Mia's visit and how her eyes lit up when she talked about the traveling merchant.

At last, I give in to my baser needs, and slide down my pants to remove my cock.

I shouldn't think of her this way. No, I absolutely shouldn't be thinking of her body, round all over. I shouldn't be thinking of her parted lips when she sucked on a candy today. But I do anyway, gently stroking myself at first, and then my hand speeding up the more I imagine licking *her* like that piece of candy.

After splattering my belly with my seed, I pull up a big blanket to cover myself and hide my shame.

She would never see me that way, my Mia, my sunshine girl. I'm a big, ugly, frightening ogre, and I think there's little I could do to convince her otherwise.

But that doesn't matter. I will stay here on my mountain to

keep watch. After everything Mia has done for me, protecting her is the one thing I'll do until the end of time.

Chapter 2

Mia

I always hate leaving Cragnorr behind. I imagine that he's lonely in his cave, but he seems content to live out his days isolated there, as much as I wish for more for him. What if there's an ogress out in the world just waiting for her partner to come along?

This sends a surprising surge of jealousy through me as I lie in bed that night. But no, I shouldn't feel that way. I should want Cragnorr's happiness, so I ponder what else I could do to bring some joy and excitement to his life. Maybe I should get him a pet. A cat would do well up there, I think, chasing down the shrews and voles that live on the mountain. I'll have to keep my eyes peeled for a new litter of kittens.

I spend the next morning helping my mother put the finishing touches on her latest rug. It will sell for a lot if she can find the right buyer for it. In the afternoon we set about to packing up her stall, because tomorrow we'll head for the market in the larger town of Sackett to sell her current inventory. It'll take two days to get there, then a day to sell, with another two days to get back home.

I'll have to warn Cragnorr tonight that I'm going away so he doesn't worry about me. I hate leaving him for so long, but I can't reasonably refuse my mother, either.

But by that evening, I'm exhausted, far more than I should be after an average day. I know I need to climb the mountain to see Cragnorr, that he's been alone in his cave, but my body feels far too heavy. Soon, just standing upright makes my head spin, and I have to lie down to keep from falling over.

He won't worry if I don't come today. I'll see him tomorrow, when I feel better—first thing in the morning, before Mom and I leave for market.

As I lie in bed, I shiver even though I'm anything but cold. Sweat beads on my forehead as if I've been running all day. That night, my dreams are strange and fearsome, filled with faceless eyes and mouths, all of them sneering and laughing.

In the dream, I'm terrified, so I call out Cragnorr's name. If anyone can help me, it's him. If anyone can protect me from the eyes, it would be my ogre.

But I'm all alone, and no one is coming to help me as I thrash and sweat beneath the blankets.

Cragnorr

It is not uncommon for a day to pass without a visit from Mia. The sting of missing her is still there, but I've grown accustomed to it. She has a life in the village, and I know that I'm an additional burden on her heart and her conscience.

Still, I watch over the cliffside all evening, waiting to see if perhaps she's running late. But there's no sign of her. She must have had a busy day.

The following morning, I do my chores, hiking to the waterfall that pours fresh water into a pool. I refill my water skins and carry them back to the cave. I've been scraping some leather, too, though I'm not sure what I intend to make with it. Perhaps a nice bag for Mia when she climbs the mountain, since she always likes to bring me things.

As afternoon passes, I resume work on a smaller chair I've been building so she has a more comfortable place to sit when she visits, and her feet will be able to touch the floor. By the time the sun is getting low in the sky, though, my worry creeps back. It's rare that she goes more than a whole two days without stopping by to pay a visit. Even if she's going out of town with her mother, she always lets me know.

I rub my tusks, trying to stave off my anxiety. Perhaps I am not as important to her as I once was. I can't deny that Mia has grown into an adult right in front of me. She's of marrying age as far as humans are concerned, because her father has mentioned it to her in passing that perhaps she should find a nice village man to settle down with. What if there's someone she likes very well and she doesn't want to tell me the truth? I've always known the day would come eventually that she would become a grown woman with grown woman's needs. There's no reason she won't have a family of her own. Perhaps that day has finally come.

As I curl up in my pile of furs that night, I feel cold despite the relatively warm weather. She wouldn't simply stop visiting me without at least explaining herself first, would she? There must be a good reason she hasn't come. I won't worry myself, not yet, about what's keeping her away.

But it's impossible not to wonder, and hope that she's all right.

MIA

The next morning, my head is swimming and my body is a terrible combination of too hot and too cold. My mother has determined I'm running a fever, and while she tries all sorts of remedies to bring it back down, I continue to sweat and shake and moan in bed.

What will Cragnorr think? I didn't visit him last night, and there's surely no way I can go to visit him today with how terrible I feel. I wish I could send Mom or Dad to let him know I'm all right, but that's impossible.

As the aching in my body grows worse and the fever drags me further down into the earth, I wonder if I'll ever even see him again.

I fall asleep when it's light out and wake when it's dark. My mother tries to feed me something, a piece of bread, but my stomach instantly revolts. The bread comes back up and I'm drained again until I fall asleep. Though everything is a blur, I can make out when a healer is brought to the house and I'm forced to drink foul-smelling liquids that are much too thick.

I have no concept of how much time has passed when, finally, the fog in my head has cleared enough that I can see what's in front of me. My skin itches where sweat has dried, and my stomach is a hollow pit.

After locating a jug of water on the bedside table and chugging half of it, I finally sit up straight. My limbs still hurt and I sway a little, but now I can move. The house is quiet, and eventually I slide out of bed. It's late afternoon now, almost evening, by the color of the light outside my window.

Oh, do I need to eat something. I need it right this moment or I might never be whole again. As I leave the room and support myself on the wall, I can make out the faint sound of many voices coming from outside.

I make my way to the front door and grab a coat to put over my nightgown before peering out.

In the main plaza, it looks like half the town has gathered, carrying lamps and torches as the sun sets. My mother is among them, talking to my father.

"Mia!" My mother rushes over when she sees me. "Oh, dear, why are you up and about? You should be in bed."

She tries to lead me back inside, but I resist her. "What's going on out here?"

A worried frown comes over her face. "Old Davon saw an ogre out in the woods. It was very close to the village, but he managed to scare it off with one of his dogs." She narrows her eyes. "It's still out there, maybe even close enough to attack."

Oh, no. My throat closes. Cragnorr has come looking for me.

"Why is everyone gathered?" I ask cautiously, already formulating my plan. I need to find him before they do, and warn him to go back to his cave.

"A search party. Everyone is going to fan out in teams and look for the monster."

I swallow hard. These are people prepared to kill, with guns in their belts and axes in their hands.

"Don't do it," I tell her, shaking her arms. "That ogre hasn't done anything to anyone. They have to stop."

The fever clearly still has the tips of its claws in me, because I feel frantic and hot.

"It hasn't done anything *yet*," my mother says. "What's gotten into you? You really should go back to bed."

I shake my head furiously and push past her, out into the street. She calls my name, but I don't stop. The assembled villagers are splitting off into groups, readying to go on the search. I'm about to call to my father, to ask him to leave the ogre alone, when I realize what a fruitless attempt that would be.

Our world has been ravaged by the trollkin. In the last war, neighboring towns were razed to the ground, so of course the village people hate anything that isn't human. Trolls, orcs, ogres— they are all simply *the enemy*.

Instead of trying to convince my father to go home, I turn around and head the other way. I'm still unsteady on my feet, but I can jog fast enough that perhaps, I can find Cragnorr before they do. Mom calls after me, but I ignore her as I leave the main street and slip between two houses, heading toward the forest.

"Cragnorr?" I call out as I pass the last home and dive into the trees. "Cragnorr!"

I have to beat them. I can't let my ogre get cut down like his parents were. I can't find him on the ground, covered in his own blood.

The only place I can think to look is the old shed where Cragnorr lived when he was young. Brambles have grown up around it, but some have been torn away from the door. I pull on the handle as hard as I can, but the fever made me weak.

"Cragnorr," I whisper, shaking the door. "It's me. It's me!"

The door opens so fast that the hinges squeal. In the doorway stands my mountain, with his big tusks framing his face, his bare chest heaving, his lower body only barely covered like it always is. His eyes are wild as he takes in the sight of me.

Then he kneels down, grabs me around the middle, and yanks me tight against him.

CHAPTER 3

CRAGNORR

I stewed alone in my cave for four days, turning over in my mind all the terrible things that could have possibly happened to Mia, when I finally couldn't stand it anymore. What if she needed me? What if someone hurt her and I wasn't there to keep her safe?

I couldn't stand the *not knowing*. What if she were taking her last breaths and I wasn't with her?

But then I encountered the man with the dogs, who shouted and ran when he saw me. They're going to keep looking for me, and I still need to find Mia. So I wait for the sun to set, wedging myself in among the various dusty belongings now occupying my old shed, where I lived out many years of my childhood. My stomach is shredded with worry—not over whether the humans will find me, but what would happen to Mia if they did. If they cut me down, how would she feel when she found out?

So I sit and wait, until suddenly, someone scrabbles at the door. Has one of their dogs tracked me?

"Cragnorr!" comes a small voice. I wonder, for a moment, if I'm imagining things. It's Mia on the other side. "It's me. It's me!"

I throw open the door, and there she is, dressed in nothing but a long gown and a coat thrown over the top. Before I can stop myself I've dropped onto my knees in front of her.

She's here. My Mia.

I wrap her tight in my arms, too overwhelmed at the familiar sight of her to remember that we don't hug anymore. She smells just like I remember, except with a hint of sickliness.

She's alive. I'm more grateful for that than anything.

After clutching her close for a few heavy moments, I release her. Mia stares up at me, her face creased in worry.

"What are you doing here?" she demands. "You shouldn't have come down from the mountain."

But I had to come. She hadn't visited in days. I had to make sure she—

"I was just sick," she says, knowing exactly what I'm thinking, like she always does. "I'm sorry. I had no way to tell you."

She does look rather ill. It must have taken her a lot of strength to come find me here.

Shouts echo outside the shed, and dogs bark. I pull the door closed quietly, wrapping myself around Mia so we can both fit into the shed now filled with junk. She lets out a tiny squeak when she bumps into a cupboard and it pushes her even closer to me, molding her small, soft body into the hard bulges of mine.

This is, of course, the moment my cock wakes up. Too many times have I thought about her underneath her clothes for it to stay quiet at the sensation of her plush body against me.

Outside the shed, voices shout at one another. Torches cast orange flashes through the windows as villagers rush past. Mia is tense, gripping my forearm and leaning into me as we both hope no one thinks to check here.

Then the barking passes, fading into the woods. The lights grow dimmer and dimmer until they vanish behind tree trunks.

Mia exhales and falls against me. She's panting like she's run a mile, and doesn't seem to be able to hold herself up. I take her hands to keep her from falling, then draw her against myself to support her weight.

After a long silence, I finally reach down to brush her hair away from her face. Her cheeks are bright red, and she can't get back to her feet.

"I'm just not feeling well," Mia says when I tilt my head. She shivers. "And I'm cold."

She should go home. She shouldn't be here when she's ill. I feel like an idiot for coming down so she had to leave her bed to come find me.

"I'm sorry," I whisper, my words coming out ground-up and harsh. They are unpracticed and unused.

"Hey," Mia says, squeezing one of my big fingers in her hand. "Don't be. You didn't know what was going on." She offers me a smile. "You were worried, weren't you?"

I nod. Of course I was. Without Mia in the world, it would forever be dark. I had no choice but to find my sunshine.

"Thank you," she says. Then she takes a deep breath and manages to get back to her feet. I don't let go of her hand, though, to keep her steady. "We need to get you out of here."

Mia

I don't think Cragnorr's cave is even safe for him now that the village knows he's here. They'll look for him everywhere. What a pickle he's gotten us into, though I understand why he did it. Now we just have to get him out safely.

But then what? Where does he go if he can't go home? Where do *I* go if I can't be with Cragnorr?

I can't think about that right now. We just have to get away from this mob.

After it's been silent for some time, I test the door to the shed and it opens with a squeak of the hinge. I wait to see if anyone's looping back, but all I can hear are the distant voices of the search parties as they fan out.

"Let's go," I whisper to Cragnorr, tugging on his hand. I step out of the shed first. Behind me, Cragnorr hunches over as small as he can and wiggles through the door, out into the open.

"We should stay close to the village," I say. "The others are out in the forest. They won't expect us here."

Uncertainly, Cragnorr nods, then follows along behind me.

We move through the darkness, our way lit only by the lamplight from the windows of nearby homes and the stars overhead. There is too much excitement and activity for anyone to notice us.

When we reach the edge of town, though, we're faced with taking the main road or the woods to either side of it. Even at night we can't go down the main thoroughfare or risk running into someone, but in the woods, we run a higher risk of getting caught by townspeople rampaging around the forest with their torches.

I'm weak and panting again. I've been lying in bed with no food in my belly for the last four days, and my energy is nonexistent. I nearly topple over, until Cragnorr reaches out to steady me.

I should let him go on alone. I'm only going to slow him down and make this more complicated. I need food and water and clothes. But then I think of those armed men out there, and I can't stand the idea of sending Cragnorr off by himself. He'll simply get caught then butchered like his parents were, whether it's at the hands of these villagers or someone else later.

Even if he manages to outmaneuver the search parties, my

sweet ogre has no idea what's out there in the world beyond his cave. I've visited other towns with my mother to sell wares so I have a lay of the land, but Cragnorr has nothing and no one except for me. He's in human territory now. He's helpless on his own.

Abruptly, Cragnorr leans down and slides one hand under my knees, then the other under my shoulders, and swings me up into his arms. I hold in my squeak of surprise, clinging to him tight as he lifts me high off the ground.

"You're going to *carry* me?" I ask, and he nods firmly, resolved. Bringing me close to his chest, he clutches me as if I weigh nothing and starts off into the woods.

In the distance, dogs are barking and men are shouting, "Ogre! Ogre!" I catch glimpses of their torches between the tree trunks. Cragnorr keeps low, his shoulders hunched, and weaves quickly through the forest despite my extra weight. I wrap my arms around his neck to hold on tighter, even though he'd never drop me. No, I'm terrified of what happens if they find us.

"Let's stay close to the road," I tell him. "They won't be looking for us here. But keep to the trees, okay?"

Cragnorr nods in agreement. He walks quickly, and at this pace, we might just make it past the mob.

That's when I hear a dog barking uncomfortably close by. It barks louder and louder, and some twigs snap.

"Run!" I tell Cragnorr, clinging onto him. "Run!"

Immediately his steps speed up, and he holds me even closer as he barrels onward. Branches catch in my hair as he sprints, but the barking behind us grows closer.

Then a gunshot rings out. I cover my ears and duck, wedging myself even deeper into Cragnorr's chest. Someone's seen us. Whoever it is, they'll have to reload before they can shoot again, but that doesn't buy us much time.

Suddenly, the barking is on top of us, and Cragnorr lets out a roar of pain. A dog has latched onto him, and he nearly trips and falls. Despite the snarling dog trying to tear the muscle out of his calf, my ogre sets me on the ground without dropping me. Then he turns around and shakes his leg frantically, trying to loosen the dog's grip.

Another shot rings out, and Cragnorr bellows. The shot must have hit his shoulder by the blood that's suddenly pouring down his arm.

"No!" I cry out, dragging myself up to my feet. Cragnorr seizes the dog around the head and yanks the creature off. He hurls it away into the brush, stunning it.

That's when two men break through the trees, guns raised. One is feverishly packing another shot, while the other grins widely.

"Found you, ogre," he snarls, exchanging his gun for a hatchet at his hip. He pulls it free and charges toward Cragnorr, weapon outstretched.

But my ogre has nothing—no way to defend himself except his hands and legs.

"Stop!" I shout as the man slashes with his axe. But Cragnorr is shockingly fast. He dodges, then reaches out and grabs the man by the arm. All it takes is one effortless swing for Cragnorr to haul the man up into the air, then slam him into the nearest tree trunk, sending him crumpling to the ground.

Still, Cragnorr's lost valuable time. The other man with the gun has reloaded, and now aims the long barrel at Cragnorr. Even worse, we've attracted the attention of the other search parties, and the sound of voices is getting closer by the second.

At last, I'm up on my feet, and I stumble towards the man with the gun with my arms held up. He freezes when he sees me.

"Mia?" he asks, dumbfounded.

I walk in front of Cragnorr, blocking his body with mine.

"Don't," I beg, recognizing the man as one of our neighbors across the street who lives with his wife. "Please. He's my friend."

"Friend?" Davon lowers his brows and raises the gun again. "Step out of the way, Mia. You don't know what you're talking about. This creature is dangerous."

"He's not!" While Davon hesitates, I crouch down and snatch the other man's hatchet up off the ground. Davon readies his gun, pointing it right at Cragnorr's head.

No. I will not let anyone hurt him. He's been bitten and shot, all while trying to protect me. I will never let them touch him again, not while I live.

So I lunge. I intend only to knock the gun out of Davon's hand, but my movements are uncoordinated and the big axe is unwieldy. The sharp edge sinks into his arm, mostly severing his hand. Blood spurts out, and the hand falls limp as his gun tumbles to the ground.

Davon lets out an ear-piercing howl.

"Go!" I holler at Cragnorr, stumbling from the effort of swinging the axe. "Run!"

His eyes are wide and panicked. But then, he narrows them in determination, and picks me up once more. He crushes me against his body, blood streaming down his arm and onto my nightgown as he turns and runs.

The man's shrieks of agony follow us on the air as Cragnorr sprints through the woods. Luckily, all the wailing has drawn the search parties in, creating a perfect distraction as we leave them behind.

I can't believe myself. My own neighbor—I've hurt him permanently, in a way that will never be fixed. I burrow into Cragnorr's sweating chest as he carries me far away, far from the village where I'll never be able to return home.

I think of my mother and father, who will hear about what I've done, what I did to Davon to save an ogre's life.

I can't go back now. I'd be thrown in jail, or worse, hanged. And maybe I deserve it.

I wonder if I'll ever see my family again. Once they hear what I've done... I'll be dead to them.

CHAPTER 4

CRAGNORR

My Mia. She defended me valiantly, and once again I owe her my life.

My Mia. Even when she could barely hold herself up on two legs, she attacked another human—for *me*.

I hold her even closer as I dodge tree trunks and low branches, as I barrel through brambles, scratching up my legs, because I know what this means.

Now we are both on the run. What she did is irreversible, unforgivable, in the minds of the villagers. She protected an ogre, a monster, and harmed one of her own.

Our fates are tied together even more deeply now as we both flee the place where we can never return. All because of me.

I run and run, despite the searing pain in my shoulder and the aching of the dog bite in my leg. The gunshot only grazed me, thankfully, and it looks worse than it is. But we must put as much distance between ourselves and the village as possible before the sun rises and men can ride out on horses to continue the search.

"Cragnorr." I don't realize I've come to a stop, my eyes starting to close, until I hear Mia's voice. "Let's find somewhere to hide. You need rest."

I shake my head. I can't rest, not while we're in danger. Not while *she* is in danger. But then her small hand cups my cheek, and her dark brown eyes look steadily into mine.

"Stop. Please. You can't go on any longer. And your arm..." She gives the wound a worried glance.

She is right that I'm losing strength quickly, so I nod in agreement. I don't know where we could possibly find shelter so far from the mountain I used to call home, but I'll try.

Still carrying Mia close to my chest, I search and search, until I find a dense patch of aspen trees huddled tightly together. Setting Mia on the ground, I break a few tree branches to open up our way inside. There's not much room in the tiny glade, but it will do for a few hours.

I go in first and cross my legs, which are unfortunately so large they take up all of the ground space. Mia chews her lip for a moment before she steps through, then neatly settles herself in the nest made by my thighs and knees.

Right then, I'm thankful that I'm too tired for even my cock to awaken. When she leans against me, though, using my chest and belly like a bed, it's much more difficult to keep it at bay. Still, I manage to quiet myself. When Mia shivers, I curl one arm around her just enough to cover some of her exposed body.

She's only out here in her nightgown because of me. Because I was foolish, because I came down to look for her when she had explicitly told me not to.

"I'm sorry," I murmur again, before I give in to sleep.

Mia

I don't blame Cragnorr for what happened. I was the one who swung that axe and did such an ugly, horrible thing. Now Davon is maimed, permanently, and I can never undo it. I'm the one who banished myself forever.

There's no turning back, so now what? Where do I go if I can't go home?

These thoughts keep me awake even as Cragnorr falls into a deep slumber. His body is warm, so warm, and feels quite wonderful. I snuggle into him, and his other arm wraps around me to pull me tight against him in his sleep.

Finally, I'm able to drift off, too. But in my dreams men tromp through the forest, their lamps and torches flashing through the trees. Davon is screaming, blood pouring from his stump.

Then, right in front of me, Cragnorr is cut down. His eyes roll back in his head, just like his parents' were when I found their dead bodies so long ago.

I wake up panting and sweating, and so, so hungry.

Cragnorr is awake, watching me as I blink bleary eyes. I'm sprawled across him, his arms keeping me rooted to his body. And where my legs are bent to nestle between his... something warm and thick is pressed against me. It's right where his—

I jerk away suddenly when I realize what's there, and scramble out of the copse of trees, my face flaming.

I know Cragnorr has one of *those*, of course. I bathed with him for years, until I became aware of just how big my breasts had gotten, and my mother made sure to tell me no one was to ever see them unless we were married. It gave men *ugly ideas*, she said. I didn't think my ogre would have those sorts of ideas, but I stopped getting in the water naked with Cragnorr after that. As his body grew bigger and taller, and that thing between his legs became thicker and longer, I didn't go with him to the lake at all. He was plenty old enough by then that he could bathe himself, and I didn't like how his exposed body made me feel—warm all over, almost ticklish, though no one was touching me.

Now I have that same hot-all-over, skin-too-tight feeling at the brush of Cragnorr's cock against my thigh. I know what cocks are for. Once a village boy fondled me, and as his sloppy hands covered my body, I saw how that *thing* grew bigger and strained at his pants.

It had felt wrong, even gross, for him to touch me that way while he was getting hard, so I left after one wet kiss. I didn't see him again, except in passing. Word got around that I was a *prude* because I wouldn't touch him, but I never let it bother me. It's up to me whether I want to touch someone's privates or not.

But Cragnorr's doesn't feel wrong and gross. No, that bulge makes me... excited.

Instead of fighting the cold air as I've been doing all night, I let it inside, hoping to cool the heat finding its way down between my legs. Soon Cragnorr emerges from the den of aspens where we slept, and he won't look at me.

So he's frightened of it, too—of how it reacted to me.

"I need to find some food," I say, earning his attention. I rub my stomach, which feels painfully empty. Cragnorr nods. "And we need to get you something for that gunshot." The wound is looking nastier as time goes on, and I have no way to treat it. "The nearest town is Sackett, to the east. If we're quick, maybe we can get there before news reaches them." I fist the few coins I found in my mother's coat. "Then I'll buy us some food there."

Cragnorr's face hardens with resolve, and together, we start walking.

That day, we manage only to find a few berries and nuts, just enough to give me some strength back. It's hard for us to get far with how wobbly I am on my feet, so Cragnorr still has to carry me a good way, which I resist because of his injury, but he won't have it. I hope neither of his wounds are getting infected.

Our stomachs are both empty as the sun sets. We decide to sleep out in the open now that we're farther away from my village, hoping the townspeople aren't still out looking for us—or worse, lawmen.

Unfortunately, I'm freezing in just my nightgown and coat, so I curl up close to Cragnorr's side on the grassy ground. He turns to face me, and I'm presented once again with his thick chest, all dense muscle with a thin layer of fat over the top to protect him. His skin is warm and soft against my face, so I wriggle even closer, and he inhales sharply. Then Cragnorr wraps his arms around me, and brings my feet between his thick legs to keep them warm.

This time, when he thickens up under his pants, I try to ignore it. He's not making any untoward movements, so what's happening must be involuntary. If he does nothing, then I'll do nothing, too. Perhaps it'll go away.

Still, it's oddly thrilling to know he feels like this about me. Does his body really want mine? Is that what it means? Does he see me as someone who he could... do that with?

Fire spreads across my body at the thought. He has a cock, and I have a place where it could go.

But he's my friend, my confidante, the person closest to me in the world. He's also an ogre, and quite a bit bigger than any human man would be.

It all seems ridiculous—in my head, anyway. My body has made completely different decisions about what it thinks of this situation we've found ourselves in. He's so warm and comforting around me that it wants to grind my hips against his, to feel even more of that thing against me. My hands itch to reach out and touch it, to find out everything about it. The fact that it belongs to Cragnorr makes it safe. Where the idea of that village boy's cock made me nauseated, I only feel anticipation now.

"Cragnorr?" I venture, afraid of disturbing the silence. He tilts his head down at me, and his eyes are always so soft, it's as if he's looking at the moon in his hand.

I wonder if asking is really the right thing to do. Maybe we would be crossing a line between us that shouldn't ever be crossed, and we won't be able to go back afterwards.

But I have no home, and neither does he. It's just the two of us out here in the wilderness, with nothing to our names but a few coins and empty hollows in our bellies. What else do I have to fear? Can I have this one good thing in the midst of the madness?

I suppose I could be afraid that Cragnorr will leave me. That's the worst thing that might happen. But I know he would never. No, Cragnorr is the only one who is truly safe, who can give me the comfort I need now that I've lost everything.

So I finally ask him, "Can I touch you?" I need another body close to mine. I need Cragnorr.

He blinks those amber eyes at me, as if he doesn't understand the words. So I place one hand on his chest and slide it down, over his stomach, to the place where a leather tie keeps his pants secured around his hips. I run my palm down farther until I'm almost to that bulge between his legs, and Cragnorr lets out a gasp.

"Here?" I ask again. My curiosity is aflame, wanting to know what's underneath, what it looks like now, and what it might feel like in my hand.

Cragnorr's mouth bobs open, his big lower jaw protruding even more than usual and pulling his big tusks away from his cheeks. Then, with wide eyes, he very slowly nods.

My heart speeds up. He wants me to do it. This fills me with far more confidence than I deserve as I try to untie the leather strap holding his pants on his big body. Then his hands land on mine, stilling them. Cragnorr uses his own his thick fingers to slip the knot free, but before he can pull his pants down, his eyes lock on mine. He wears a worried frown, like he's afraid of me seeing him —and perhaps not liking what I find.

"You're safe with me," I tell him, smoothing one hand up his arm to his big tusk. I stroke it from base to tip, and he shudders under me. Then, with a grunt of agreement, he tugs his pants down.

That hidden thing practically springs out, like an animal desperate to be free of a cage. Seeing it sends a bolt of lightning right from my throat to the crux of my thighs, which I unconsciously clench together.

Cragnorr's cock is huge, even more than I expected. It's growing in front of my eyes, the wrinkled, green skin smoothing out and stretching as the inside fills up larger. There's something soft and round hidden under the skin at the tip, and tentatively, I reach out to touch it.

Cragnorr inhales sharply when I sweep my hand over his hot flesh. His cock surges, leaning into my palm, so I touch it again, this time wrapping my fingers partway around him.

"Mia," Cragnorr whispers, and his hips tremble. It's so rare for him to speak that I'm encouraged, and I squeeze a little more, earning a pleased gasp.

But I'm not sure what to do with it now. I decide to explore, stroking my hand downward to pull that wrinkled skin back and expose what's underneath. It reveals a soft, mushroom-shaped head with a slit in the middle that bisects it, and it's an even darker green compared to the rest of him. This time Cragnorr rewards me with an actual moan, and it's most certainly a sound of pleasure.

The ogre who has barely spoken in his life is moaning under my hand, and I feel immeasurably powerful.

I bring my hand up to surround the head again, shrouding it

before I stroke down, squeezing gently. Cragnorr's fingers, which have been resting on my shoulder until now, clench. He's panting, so I slide my hand up again, then bring my other hand to wrap the rest of the way around him.

When I pull that skin back, drawing my grip down to the root, he rewards me with a full-throated groan that sets a fire spreading across my skin.

Then I discover something curious. His cock is now full and thick, and has a prominent ridge running down the underside that leads to a big sac. It's got dark hair on it like the hair around the base of his length, and each time I stroke, it twitches and draws up. Tentatively I explore down with one hand, and Cragnorr rewards me with more groans when I cup him gently. I find two rather large objects inside, and when I massage there, his hips jerk. His eyes find mine and they are simply wild, his pupils huge and black, swallowing up all of his iris. His teeth are clenched and now his hands are stroking me in return, up and down my sides, over my hips and back again. I love how he feels touching me all over, and I want even more of it.

I return to his cock and pump him faster, never breaking our eye contact. But soon Cragnorr can't help it any longer and his eyes fall closed, his head tipping back, and he lets out a guttural sound as his cock swells in my hand.

If I thought it was big before, it doesn't compare to now. The whole thing fills up and then, suddenly, white liquid shoots out, right at my chest. It paints my night gown across the collar bone, and then more spurts down my breasts. My hands abruptly stop as even more of it leaks out, spilling over my wrists.

When Cragnorr finally opens his eyes, he sees what he's done, and his expression turns frantic. He tries to wipe the creamy white stuff away, but there's not really any helping it.

I laugh. It just comes out of me, and I have to cover my mouth to stop it. Cragnorr's shoulders curl up to his neck, as if he's afraid I'm making fun of him.

I pat his arm. "It's all right," I say, cleaning as much off with my hand as I can and wiping it on the grass. "I was dirty anyway."

CHAPTER 5

CRAGNORR

I can't believe it.

When Mia took my cock in her hands, it felt nothing like my own clumsy grip. No, it was soft and tentative at first, until she realized what she could do.

I've never known a creature to wield such vast power. And then, like an idiot, I shot my come all over her.

For a moment, I don't feel tired or hungry. I can't feel the ache in my shoulder or in my leg. I feel nothing but a warm sense of joy, all the way down to my balls. Mia is here with me, in my arms. I can't help but feel that she belongs here, wedged against my body. I feel a quietude, a peace I've never known before. And that magic she wove with her fingers... I could die right now, and I would know I've lived the happiest moment of my life.

She touched me. *She* wanted to touch *me*. Now she's curled up in my arms and I'm still dazed, absently rubbing circles on her skin.

What am I thinking? Why didn't I touch her back? She showed

me a world of pleasure, and I didn't even think to return the favor. I was too lost in my stupor. When I look down at her, though, Mia's fallen asleep, her hands curled up on my chest.

I sigh and lie back in the grass, holding her tight against me. She shifts, and already my cock is thinking about her again. Not just what her fingers feel like—but what other parts of her might feel like, too. I wonder if she would let me touch her the way she touched me? What would I find between her thighs?

There are bigger things to worry about, like whether we can reach the next town in time, if the villagers are still on our trail, if we'll find enough food to survive. But I fall asleep thinking of Mia's curves, soft and giving under my hands.

I awake the next morning first again, Mia still sleeping soundly. She rolled off me in the night, and now lies bundled up in the nook of my arm. I'm wrapped around her, dwarfing her, but thankfully not crushing her. The wound in my shoulder is pressed against the ground, which is deeply uncomfortable, but I refuse to move for many long minutes.

As I watch her chest swell and give with her breaths, I'm dying to know what's under her nightgown. Soon my hands start exploring her, drifting from her back down to her hip, then up her side. I know I shouldn't, but after the gift she gave me... I can't help myself.

She burrows even more deeply into me, making a pleased sound. I trail my fingers down until they're skating over her thighs, but stop when she gasps.

Now she's awake.

"Keep going," she says as she takes my big thumb in her hand. "More."

More?

Of course I can't deny Mia anything. And if what she wants is my touch, I'll more than happily give it to her.

She guides my hand up her thigh to her butt, and my breath hitches as I caress the gentle swell of it. She leans into me, her hip rising off the ground to make even more contact.

Oh, my cock is certainly alert now. Continuing my exploration, my fingers duck under her arm, and she lifts it for me to grant me access to her chest. There, I'm stopped in my tracks by the perfect plushness of her breast. It's much larger than I expected, and surprisingly full and heavy. I wonder what it feels like to carry this around all day; I want nothing more than to lift it and ease the burden for her.

"It's all right," Mia whispers, turning her body to make my way easier. My pants feel terribly tight as I touch the rounded bottom of her breast, then travel up and across a hard, pebble-sized peak. Her breath catches as I brush over it, so I do it again, and she lets out a pleased sigh.

This time I bring the little bead between my fingers and gently pinch it, curious what it will do. Mia's eyes close and her whole body arches, which seems like a good sign. I repeat it with her other breast, too, cupping both of them in my palms while I play with these two tantalizing points.

My cock is hungry, painfully hungry, while I tease her. It wants something else, but I'm not sure what.

When I've paid sufficient attention to her breasts, I wander with my hand once again, intent on discovering every part of Mia while she'll allow it. I remember once upon a time being fascinated with the space between her legs. She didn't have a cock there, like I do—no, it was something hidden, something much more special. Will she let me touch her there and find out?

I run my hand down her belly to the triangle where her pelvis and thighs come together. Mia lets out a little squeak, and I pause, not sure if she wants me to continue.

Then she grabs my hand in hers and pushes it between her thighs, where it catches on her nightgown.

My whole body gets warm just imagining what I'll find there, in this secret place.

MIA

My body is simply tingling, my blood all rushing to my nipples and my abdomen. When Cragnorr reaches down there, my pussy clenches tight, craving his hands.

I'm elated that he wants to touch me in return. He wants to know me, explore me, and I'm more than happy to let him as he let me.

I pull up my nightgown and part my thighs. His hand slips through them, but at first, all he does is knead my flesh. I whine a little, shifting until just the pad of his finger tastes me.

It's such a slight movement, but it sends a shockwave from where he's touching me straight up to my throat. I gasp as he gently strokes the outside of me, teasing my lower lips. Then he slides between them, and meets moisture there. Cragnorr's amber eyes go wide as he encounters this new discovery. That slickness allows his finger to slide up between my folds, where he finds my sensitive clit, which I've often touched at night to pleasure myself. I moan into his chest, and he pauses.

"More," I say, pushing on his wrist again. "Please."

Obediently he repeats the gesture, passing over that sensitive nub again with the pad of his finger.

"Yes," I murmur. "Like that."

With a firm nod, Cragnorr continues tantalizing me, rubbing back and forth and then around in circles. Soon I'm wriggling under his hand, pushing my hips against it as I ask for even more.

My pussy clenches as if something is missing, but the pleasure is so wonderful that I ignore it.

Cragnorr's breaths speed up as he moves his finger faster, and soon I'm unable to control the sounds coming out of my mouth as he winds me tighter and tighter. I might just pop like a ripe fruit.

And then it hits me—an explosion of pleasure that radiates out from where he's touching me to every inch of my body. I cry out as it takes me over, all my muscles contracting. Cragnorr continues rubbing until I reach down to stop him, the sensation too much for me to bear.

"Oh, wow," I mutter against his chest, my head foggy from bliss. Slowly it clears, and I find Cragnorr looking down at me with his mouth slightly ajar. "That felt amazing."

He withdraws his hand and curiously looks at his fingers, which are coated with my wetness. First he sniffs it, much to my mortification, then slips one finger in his mouth to taste it.

"What are you doing?" I ask, embarrassed. But his eyes fall closed as he sucks on it, and pleasure spreads across his face.

"Delicious," he says quietly, opening his eyes again to peer down at me.

That's not what I expected, and again, it makes me clench between my legs. I want to touch him again, to bring him pleasure like he just brought me, but my belly hurts from how hungry I am.

At least I no longer feel dizzy and sick. Perhaps I'm finally through the worst of it.

Now it's time to go.

As we head south, toward where I believe we'll find Sackett, the landscape changes. Cragnorr's wounds are looking better, despite the conditions, and I've gotten some of my strength back.

We spot farms through the trees, and open fields with houses dotting the horizon. I don't want what happened in my village to happen again, so as the woods thin out around us, eventually I stop and turn to Cragnorr.

"You should stay here," I say. "Sackett is just ahead. I don't want anyone to see you."

He stops in his tracks and gazes down at me with a concerned look in his eyes. I know he doesn't like it, but we don't have a choice.

"Don't worry," I tell him, with more confidence than I feel. "News shouldn't have traveled here. I'll go in, get some food and come right back. All right? But I need you to wait for me."

His eyebrows lower and he frowns. The idea bothers me, too. Anything could happen to Cragnorr while I'm gone.

"Hide, please." I put a hand on his forearm and squeeze. "I need you to be safe."

After a long moment of studying me, Cragnorr nods. He returns my gesture, then pats my head before I turn around and walk away.

I pull my jacket tighter around myself when I finally find a road. The packed dirt leads me to more homes, which pull closer together as I pass. Other people appear, and they stare at me unabashedly as I walk by in only my dirty, torn nightgown and this coat over my shoulders.

At last, I reach Sackett, a town significantly larger than the village where I grew up. I've been here before with Mom to sell her rugs, so I have a rough lay of the land in my head. There's a general store on the main road, and that's where I'll go to get something to wear and hopefully, some meager food supplies.

I play with the few coins in my pocket, hoping my own village hasn't sent ahead word about me. I would be easy to recognize with my thick, long hair and curious clothes.

Finally, I reach the big shop in the middle of town, still drawing far too much attention to myself. Maybe I can't afford a new outfit, but I can at least buy some food to hold us over, plus a basic knife and a firestarter.

The shopkeep gives me a very funny look when I come in dressed as I am, but he's happy to take my money. After bagging up my purchases, he drops the coins into his till and waves me off. "Thank you," I say, before scooping it all up and heading out the door.

It's slow going back the way I came with all the eyes following me. At the edge of town, a man with a sly face stops me.

"I'll give you some clothes if you suck me off," he says, waggling his eyebrows.

I turn around and run, back the way I came—back to Cragnorr.

CHAPTER 6

CRAGNORR

When I find her, my girl has collapsed into a pile on the forest floor, a paper bag clutched in her arms. Tears stream down her face, dripping all over everything. When I push through the branches, cracking off a few twigs, her head snaps up. Relief fills her face, and she drops her bag as she leaps to her feet.

"Cragnorr!" She throws herself at me, and I catch her just in time. Her arms wrap as far as they can around my barrel body while she cries into my chest. "I'm so glad you're here. There was a man in the village, and..." She trails off, her lip trembling. "I'm happy to see you."

I put my arms around her, wondering what happened to make her upset this way. I hold her until her crying has subsided, running my hand over her soft hair, threading my fingers through the thick waves. Then I rock her back and forth, cradling her until at last, she can look up at me again.

"I brought food," Mia croaks. She gets out of my lap and returns to the dropped paper bag, where some smaller bags have spilled across the forest floor. "Shit," she says. "Some of the peanuts fell out." She gathers it all up, pausing occasionally to brush tears away from her cheeks. "We're going to figure this out, okay? We'll find somewhere nice out in the woods. We'll make a camp, and we'll learn how to survive. We can do it, I know we can." She nods firmly. "If we're together, we can do anything."

I smile tentatively, hoping that she's right, because I will follow her to the end of the world if it means I get to stay by her side.

When Mia lies down on the ground, saying she's far too full to walk more, I follow suit. She slides over so her head is resting on my arm like a pillow, and sighs into my armpit.

"That was really nice," she murmurs, so quiet I almost can't hear her. "What you did this morning."

I peer down at her. She's avoiding my gaze, her hands curled up in front of her chest. I take one in my own hand and give it a gentle squeeze, because I liked it, too. Now I want even more of her. I want to show her what she means to me, how much I appreciate her and everything she's given up for me.

Right then, I decide to be bolder. If she enjoyed that, what if I brought her even more pleasure? The idea excites me.

Releasing her hand, I let my palm slide over her nipple, and Mia inhales sharply. Gently I roll it in my fingers over the fabric of her nightgown, like I did before, until she's panting and pushing her chest into my touch.

Once Mia is twitching underneath me, I leave her breast and find my way down to the hem of her nightgown. I'm more forward this time in pulling it up over her thighs, exposing her lower body to the forest. She squeaks as I seek out that soft, warm place between her legs. They open for me.

Again I explore her, sampling each part of her, and I'm drawn back over and over to that wet dip beneath her sensitive button. It's tiny, like a pinhole. I wish I knew what it was.

"You're supposed to put something in there," she murmurs.

I give her a surprised look, and she pats my cheek. Human ways are mysterious to me, but if that's what Mia wants, that's what I'll give her.

I run my finger around, exploring the small hole and marveling at how hot and wet it is. When I try to dip the pad inside her, though, she's much too small.

When I frown and try to pull my hand away, Mia stops me. "It will fit," she says. "It's... it's supposed to go there."

My eyes jump to hers. Is that so? My hand is meant to be inside her? Then I hope it will feel good.

Again I try to press into her, and this time... the tiny hole abruptly gives. Mia lets out a sharp cry, and I yank my hand back, terrified of what I've done.

Fuck. I've hurt my little human, and guilt swells up in me.

"Hey, hey." Mia strokes my tusk. "That's supposed to happen."

I stare at her, aghast. I'm meant to hurt her? That's not what I wanted. I wanted to make her drip and moan like she did before. But she takes my hand, and once more she guides it down between her legs. "It's okay, Cragnorr. I promise."

Swallowing hard, I return to touching her, experimenting with circles and rubs until she grips my shoulder and moans. Once I've pleased her there, I return southward, and find that hole is not nearly so small as before.

"Now do it," she whispers to me. I nod and press my finger in again, and this time, it breaches her. She hisses with pain, but stops my hand before I can draw it back. "Don't stop."

Mystified by this combination of emotions, I decide to obey

her, and I slide my finger in even deeper. Whatever this place is... the texture inside is marvelous, soft and spongey and slick with something that certainly isn't water. This must be what I tasted on my fingers, and that makes my cock shiver under my pants.

When I've reached as deep as I can, I withdraw, and once again bring her flavor up to my lips. There is a little blood on my hand, and I gasp in shock. Blood? Oh, no. I've injured her.

"It's normal," Mia says, patting my hair. I search her eyes for any sign that she's trying to protect my feelings, but she's smiling. So I lick my finger, tasting her again, and Mia hides her face. "I can't believe you," she says, mock-offended. But now I'm hooked on the taste of her. I need more.

Fueled by this, I take her by the shoulders and push her onto her back. "Cragnorr!" she says in surprise. I reposition myself so I'm kneeling between her legs, and then I crouch down low to bring my face to the apex of her thighs. "What are you—?" she starts to say, but she interrupts herself with a moan when I swipe my tongue across her exposed flesh.

There it is. That delicious taste that I've been craving for hours. Again, I lick her from top to bottom, and she writhes under my mouth. I sample her with my tongue, sliding it inside her and twisting it around. She enjoys this, almost as much as she enjoys me playing with that tiny bead of pleasure. Returning to it, I attack it with my mouth, chasing the moans flowing from her lips.

Right. My finger. She liked that, even if it hurt a little, so I decide to do both at the same time. It slips inside her much easier this time, and she lets out a cry as I do it.

"Oh!" Her little channel twitches around me. "That's... that's so good."

Pleased by this response, I withdraw my finger and then sink it into her again, the part she seems to like most, and she rewards me by making more noise and getting even wetter. I flick my tongue over her harder, faster, as I move my hand inside her. She's growing slicker and softer under my ministrations, opening for me. As an experiment, I wiggle another finger inside her, and Mia jerks, rocking her hips into my face with each thrust.

"Cragnorr, just like that," she whimpers, tangling her fingers in my hair. "Please!"

So I give her more. And more. Soon she's keening, her hands gripping my head, her body jerking with every one of my pumps. I test out wiggling my fingers, stroking her inside, trying to understand the texture along her upper wall. Her moans increase in volume, and suddenly her little canal squeezes tight, so tight I almost can't move my hand. A loud cry bursts out of her, and warm liquid trickles down over my palm. I withdraw it and lick her up as fast as I can.

The taste of her is marvelous. Perfect.

"Shit," Mia says, her eyes half-lidded. "What was that?"

I don't know myself. I simply let instinct guide me, her little cries and heady moans driving me towards what she wanted. Now my cock is not only awake, but drooling in my pants for something I can't quite place.

That hot, wet channel between her legs, though... oh, does it call to me. I cup it in my hand, feeling as if I've received a gift today.

"You like my pussy?" she asks, squinting as she moves. I blink at her, then smile widely.

I liked it very much, this *pussy*.

"Good. I like yours, too. Well, your cock." She gets a mischievous, feral smile on her face, and reaches for the tie of my pants. I stare in wonder as she unfastens it, then slides my pants down my hips. I'm rock hard after licking her, and she takes my length in her hands and strokes it again, like she did last night.

It's all too easy to reach my finish, and this time I make sure to angle myself away from her, painting the forest floor white.

Finally, we've recovered from our meal. "Where should we go?" asks Mia.

I shrug. I have no idea what becomes of us next.

"We should look for a place we can set up camp," Mia says. "Start a fire, maybe make some tools."

We get up and keep walking, and to our surprise, we wander across a path. It's not well-maintained, but it'll make our way much faster. Mia talks about our future camp, and surmises how we might be able to carve some rudimentary knives to start the process going.

All I can think about as we continue on is how she tasted, how she felt around my fingers, how her little moans drove me wild. I want something more, but I don't know what it is.

I'm so lost in my daydream that I don't notice when we encounter a thin rope stretched across the path. My shin bumps into a taut string, and I pause to peer down at what I've run into.

The ground suddenly moves, rising up underneath us. A net emerges from the dirt and pine needles, sweeping us both off our feet. Mia cries out as she's thrown into my body by the force of the net closing around us, and the bag of goods falls out of her hands, onto the ground. We fly up into the trees. Then we both jerk as the net suddenly stops.

The ropes bite into my back, and Mia is crushed against my side. As she curses, I try to shift so she's facing my belly, instead, and the whole thing squeaks.

"What the hell?" Mia demands, glaring up at where the net is tied to a massive tree branch overhead. It's bowing from the weight of me in the net. "What's this doing here?"

She struggles as if it will free us, so I put my hands on her shoulders to still her and shake my head. She stops, but her eyes are wide and terrified.

Who put this here, and why?

"What's happening, Cragnorr?" she says, voice fearful.

I wrap my arms around her, wishing I knew the answer.

CHAPTER 7

MIA

I can't believe this. No matter how hard we struggle, no matter how Cragnorr tries to tear the rope open with his big hands, the net doesn't budge.

I suppose I should have been more wary when we stumbled across that worn path. Whether this net was intended for humans or for game, we're now trapped.

"Damn it," I hiss, trying again to get comfortable, but it's impossible. The ropes of the net are squeezing me even through my coat, smooshing me against Cragnorr's body.

We hang like that for what feels like hours, curled up in terribly uncomfortable positions, forced to stare down at the food and supplies scattered all around the forest floor underneath us. The knife is there, just out of reach, which infuriates me more than anything. As if to taunt us, a squirrel runs out into the middle of the path and picks up a bunch of *my* peanuts, then carries them away.

We can't even get up to any foolery with how awkward we are, and every time one of us moves, the whole net shifts, which presses us into even stranger contortions.

"Is someone going to come?" I ask, adjusting my body weight yet again, which pushes me even harder against Cragnorr's chest.

He shrugs helplessly. He doesn't know, either.

I'm getting sore as the sun starts to set. I hope we aren't stuck here forever. My belly rumbles madly, and I'm so hungry that I feel like I might throw up. My mouth is dry as a bone. I try to reach down for the food where it's scattered all across the forest floor, but it creates all sorts of problems, and we're much too high up.

Cragnorr shifts his arm to take the pressure of the net off of me, but it's not enough. I can see his skin is starting to turn red where the ropes have been cutting into him.

"We caught something!" a woman's voice calls out through the woods.

I sit upright at the sound. They're coming for us, whoever set this trap. A bizarre feeling of relief falls over me. Maybe they'll free us once they realize we aren't the deer they intended to catch.

"Whoa." Two people appear, a tall woman with a thick braid and a shorter man with a pudgy middle. She carries two daggers, and he has a gun at his hip. The man is staring at us in wonder. "It's…"

"An ogre?" the woman supplies.

"Please!" I call out to them. "Please let us down! I'm sorry if we were on your land or something, it's just that we're lost, and—"

"All right, all right," the man interrupts. "Shut up." He turns to the woman. "What should we do with them?"

"Leave them for now," she says, surveying us. "We're going to need help."

"Please," I say. "We've been here all day. I promise we don't want any trouble. We're hungry, and thirsty, and—"

"What the fuck did I say?" the man roars at me, and I fall silent.

He rolls his eyes. "Yeah," he tells the woman. "The ogre is going to be a problem."

With that, they turn away and walk off into the woods.

"No!" I call out after them, panic rising up into my chest. "Come back! Let us down! Please, just give me some water!"

But they merely talk amongst themselves as they vanish.

I can't control it anymore. A sob breaks out of me, and Cragnorr strokes my hair as I fall apart.

They don't intend to free us, whoever they are. And there's nothing we can do.

CRAGNORR

It's much later that day, almost sunset, when the humans reappear. Mia has cried herself to sleep, twitching and shaking in my arms as ugly dreams haunt her. They emerge from the trees, now ten in number, with the man and woman from before among them.

Mia jolts awake, and frantically reaches out through the holes in the net. "Please," she begs. "Let us down."

"A big guy," one of the newcomers remarks, stroking his chin. They're completely ignoring her. "Good thing we brought the heavy ropes."

One of the humans, a spry one with skinny arms and legs, crawls up the tree to where the net is fixed to the branch. He pulls something, and then, we're falling.

"Oof!" Mia shouts with pain as we both land on the forest floor. One of her arms is caught underneath me, and I hope it hasn't broken. Before I can roll away, though, the net is being dragged off of us.

"Grab him!" A dozen hands seize my limbs. I try to kick them off, but they're quick, and before I can get to my feet they have ropes tied around my ankles and wrists. I thrash, but the ropes pull tight the more I move.

"Cragnorr!" calls out Mia as two men haul her up to her feet. I bellow in fury and swing one of my arms, managing to pull one of my captors off the ground.

"Shit," one of them says. "We should have brought more people."

This gives me faith for a moment that I can escape this. I roar and fling my arm forward with all my might—lifting the man holding it down right off the ground and tossing him upside-down.

A big man flings himself on top of me to pin me to the ground. "Two per arm and leg!" he shouts, and the others swarm around me like flies, two of them holding each rope. "Get him in the wagon!"

I can't move as they drag me by the hands, the others holding my legs fast. Mia stumbles, and one of her shoes falls off. "Fuck you!" she spits out, trying to escape her own bonds. "Let us go!"

I roar and thrash, but trying to escape is useless as the men and women around me yank me up into a wagon, then lash me down on my back with ropes, each tied through metal rings fastened to the sides. Mia cries out as she fights the two men holding her captive.

"What do you want?" she shouts. "You can't do this to him!"

They just laugh as they toss her into the front of the wagon, where I can no longer see her. I'm forced to stare up at the sky, at the tree branches criss-crossing overhead, not knowing what awaits us—and terrified that I can't protect Mia from it.

Mia

"Come on, you guys," I say for the fifth time, trying to pour as much sweetness into my voice as I can. "We didn't know this was your place. We would never have been using your path if we knew it belonged to someone. I promise, we're innocent."

"Make her shut up," the woman with the braids growls. Finally, one of my two captors—the terribly skinny guy who's apparently named Gru—rips off a piece of my gown and shoves it in my mouth.

I had expected this sooner or later. My mom has always called me a chatterbox.

Besides, they don't care why we're here. I tried to tell them that we have no money, that Cragnorr presents no threat to anyone, but the words washed over them like water. They laughed at me.

"The King will love this story," one of them said. "A little girl and her big strong ogre, on the run."

King? I furrow my brow, because there's only one king, and he's a dumb old oaf who lives in a castle far away, existing only to make war with the trollkin. That can't be who they're talking about, way out here.

I grumble into the scrap of fabric stuffed in my mouth as my captors prattle on. Poor Cragnorr, tied down like an animal. I turn my head to try to look at him, but one of my captors jerks on the rope binding my hands and I snap my head forward again.

What are they going to do with him?

It's almost full dark when, up in the distance, lights come into view. With the lights comes *noise*, like dozens—no, hundreds of people—are all singing and laughing and arguing at once.

We push through the trees, and I'm completely unprepared for what I see.

A *town*. It's hidden well here, surrounded on two sides by a steep hill. There are spiked logs arranged all around the outside in a wall, lit torches burning in what look like small guard towers. Up ahead, a gate opens, and the woman with the braids hails up to the guards.

"You weren't kidding," one of them calls down. "It *is* an ogre!"

"I would never lie about that," she says. "I lie about plenty of things, but not that."

Then the wagon is moving again, and we pass through the gates. Just great. There's no way I'm getting out of this place if it's guarded that well. My only choice is to talk our way out of this.

Beyond the gate is an open space with a stable off to one side. There are all sorts of wagons and carts assembled, many full of sacks and goods, while others are overflowing with vegetables, some beginning to rot. I can tell by the reek.

I'm dragged out of the wagon by my captor, Gru, and I thrash in his grip. "Stop doing that, girlie, or you'll regret it," he snarls at me, and I fall still. I don't want to know what he means by that.

Then everyone in the party stops moving and talking at once. A man approaches us, his hands folded behind his back. He's tall, with sharp, square shoulders and a trimmed goatee, his long black hair hanging down around his ears. His jacket, while brightly-colored and quite fancy, is dirty. High-waisted pants flare out around his knees before squeezing into tall leather boots, which are also filthy.

"Your Majesty," the woman with the braids says, bowing.

"Who's this?" The man pauses in front of me, then tilts his head to one side. Gru reaches into my mouth and pulls out my gag so I can answer.

"You're the King?" I ask. Maybe if I can get him to listen to reason, he'll have the power to release us.

The man turns to me, arching an eyebrow. "That would be me. You still haven't answered who *you* are."

"Look, I'm just some girl. Really. I'm not special or important or anything." I don't know what he wants with us, but I have to prove that we're not worth it. "My friend and I are just trying to survive. We didn't mean to trespass or anything, really—"

"Shut up," Gru says, yanking on my ropes. "And it's *Your Majesty.*"

"Does she always talk this much?" the King asks my captors.

"She never closes her trap," someone else says.

With a sigh, the King waves a hand at me dismissively and walks away to examine Cragnorr.

"Wait!" I call after him. "There's really no reason to hold us. We're just more mouths to feed, right? Let us go and—"

Gru slaps me across the face, and my head reels to one side. My ear is ringing when he steps away.

The King ignores us, continuing his inspection of Cragnorr. "You really found an ogre," he murmurs, and Cragnorr growls in return. I just hope he doesn't do anything to warrant them hurting him even more.

"Caught in our net in the woods," the woman says proudly.

"Please," I say again. "He's not what you think he is. He's not one of *them.*"

This supposed "king" pauses, then turns to look at me again. "You said he was your 'friend.' What does this mean? How does a human girl come to be 'friends' with an ogre?"

"He's good," I say. "He might be trollkin, but he's no danger to anyone. I promise. I've known him since he was a kid."

The King purses his lips thoughtfully. Then he turns back to Cragnorr.

"Fascinating," he says. Then he gestures at the ropes. "Take the ogre to the holding cells. He'll be a perfect addition to our arena lineup."

"What?" I demand. "We haven't done anything wrong! Why are you putting him in jail?"

The King circles back around so he's standing in front of me.

"And this chatty thing," he says, leaning forward to get a closer look at me, "I want her. Take her to the beer hall and tie her to the chair next to mine. I can't wait to find out all about my new pet."

CHAPTER 8

CRAGNORR

I roar and fight as the wagon is dragged away, leaving Mia behind. The metal rings holding me down squeak, but don't budge. She tries to run after me, until the lecherous little man next to her snatches her arm to hold her still.

"Don't take him!" she begs, fighting him, but nobody's listening. I try to flail my arms and legs to get back to Mia, but all it does is cause the ropes to bite into my flesh.

It doesn't matter. I will find her. Wherever they take me, I will escape and I will find her.

I can't see where we're going as the wagon is led away. Then the ropes around me are untied, and I sit up suddenly, trying to get my legs under me so I can make a break for it.

"No, you don't," someone says, and a massive, heavy object slams into my chest. I crumple as pain rips through my ribcage. When I can look up again, a short, stocky woman stands above me with a giant metal bar in her hands.

"Try to get away again," she says. "I dare you."

A group of large men set upon me, fastening metal clamps to my wrists and ankles, and binding my arms together behind my back. I thrash against them. I must get back to Mia. I can't let her fall into these horrible people's hands, all alone.

Then comes the cold bite of a metal collar snapping shut around my neck. It's too tight and too heavy, and I sag under it. The stout woman yanks on a chain attached to my throat, and I'm forced to stumble towards her. With a pleased grunt, she pulls me along, my prison guards following.

I have no choice but to go with her, or they might just snap my neck. Then what good would I be to Mia?

Reluctantly I follow along as I'm led down, down into the ground by a set of stairs. When my eyes finally adjust, I see where we're headed: a dark, damp room filled with metal cages, and almost half of them are occupied. I can't help staring as I pass by. There's a monster of a man inside the first cage, chained to the bars by his ankles. He's missing one eye and there's a massive scar down his face. Across from him... is an orc.

When I was still a whelp, my family traveled all over, looking for others of our kind. They intended to find more ogres like us, but more often than not we came across trollkin, who regarded us with irritation, but never aggression.

We ogres don't fight in their wars. We don't participate in their endless campaign against the humans, but we are still one of them. Orcs, ogres, trolls—we are all enemies of the humans, and that binds us together.

"An ogre?" the orc says, rising to his feet as I'm led past. I don't know much Trollkin anymore, as I haven't spoken it since my parents died, but I recognize enough to understand him.

There's also a troll woman down here, and another human man who appears to be nothing but bone and muscle. The trolless approaches the edge of her cage as I'm led to the one next to her.

"Just great," she says in Trollkin, leaning back against the bars. "He's fucking huge."

The stout woman leading me by my chain raps on the bars of the trolless's cage with her huge metal baton, filling the room with a terrible metallic ring. "Silence!" she shouts. Then she unlocks the door of the empty cage in front of us and points into it. "Get in," she says to me, raising her weapon. The other men still stand behind her, ready to pounce should I try to escape.

No, I can't make my move now, not while I'm surrounded. But they'll have to take me out of this cage eventually, and perhaps if I've shown compliance, they'll let their guard down enough for me to escape.

Obediently I step inside the cage, and the chain linked to my neck is snapped into a metal ring on the floor just beyond the bars.

They're afraid of me, I realize. None of the others here are chained down the way I am, restricted from hardly any movement at all.

The cage door is slammed closed and the key turned in the lock. I'm trapped.

Mia

As Gru drags me along behind him through the small town, I observe what I can, because it's all information I can use later.

A main thoroughfare leads away from the front gates, into a scattered mess of tents and rickety wooden structures, all slapped together at odd angles. We pass two men locked in a drunken brawl, and I cringe as one of them smashes a fist into the other's jaw. It cracks, and some onlookers cheer. Other people gather around fire pits, sharing bowls of soup along with their mugs of mead or beer. Many of them have gold piercings, scars in obvious places, and bedraggled clothes just as filthy as the king's.

Where have we found ourselves?

Deeper in the camp, Gru leads me to an immense tent held up by massive wooden posts, with half a dozen huge tables. The tables are already half-full of people, and the noise inside the tent is almost deafening. At the head of the center table, my captor pulls out a chair and shoves me into it. Then he ties my hands around the back of the chair so I can't even consider moving.

"There," he says with a nod of approval, then takes his own seat farther down. All I can do now is wait.

More people stream into the tent, taking seats with mugs in their hands and throwing their feet up on the tables. It's like not a single one of them has a sense of decorum. Someone eats a big turkey leg a few seats down from me and spits out the gristle, right on the table. A beer is knocked over when two people start arm wrestling.

When the King enters, a wild cheer goes up from the assembled crowd. The revelers bang their mugs on the wooden tables and hoot like wild animals as he passes, until he reaches me. He pauses for a long moment, surveying me, before a terrible smile creeps across his face.

"Rather beautiful for a village girl," he says, leaning down to get a closer look. He grabs my chin in his hand, forcing me to look right and then left as he studies me. I yank my head away and he chuckles. It's a hollow sound deep in his throat that reminds me of a dog's growl. "And feisty. Even more fun to break."

I swallow at this last word, but endeavor to keep the fear off my face as the King circles around behind me, taking a seat in the big, elaborate chair at the head of the table.

"You don't have to break me," I say, waving my hands. "Really, no breaking necessary."

But he ignores me. When he holds up his arms, the room falls quiet.

"Look who we found tromping through our woods!" he calls out, gesturing widely at me. "And do we tolerate trespassers?"

"No!" the assembled people call out, banging their mugs on the tables.

"I didn't know I was trespassing!" I struggle in my chair, but the ropes bite into my wrists. "I wouldn't have gotten anywhere near your crazy town if there had been a *sign*, at least—"

"And such a mouth on her!" he roars. Boos rise up from the crowd. "Normally I would call for her death…" I blanch. Death just for trespassing? "But given that I am without a queen, I might keep her."

Peals of laughter rise up from the crowd. "A queen?" someone barks. "This stranger?"

I can't hide my disgust. I would bite and claw him before I'd let him get his hands on me and make me his *queen*.

The king holds up a hand to stop the objections. "You misunderstand me. She's a toy to tide me over until my queen arrives." He hooks his foot around my chair and drags me closer, until he can sling an arm over my shoulders. My whole body shivers with repulsion. "Every king needs a plaything, doesn't he?"

Nods of agreement ripple down the tables. I try to pull away, but his arm is like iron.

"Let me go," I hiss. "I'll rip off your balls."

He ignores me. "In two days' time…" He raises his mug into the air. "We will have another fight!"

The crowd whoops and crows. "A fight! A fight!" they roar.

I wonder what kind of fight he means.

"Until then," the king calls out over the din, "drink, fuck, make merry, and prepare for our next raid!"

Applause fills the tent, and I sink lower into my chair. All my muscles tense, and I glance at the king from the corner of my eye.

I can only hope *fucking* isn't what he has planned for me. I couldn't do it, not after what I shared with Cragnorr. He's the only one who can touch me that way.

I hope he's safe, wherever he is, and that they haven't decided to hurt or torture him. What do they want with my ogre?

What will they do to him?

CRAGNORR

Once I was brought in and caged, silence fell among the other captives. Now that the stout woman with the baton is gone, though, they try to talk to me.

"How'd you get caught, ogre?" It's the big orc asking in Trollkin.

I shrug. It would take far too long to explain. I would have to tell him what Mia means to me, why I came down the mountain when I shouldn't have, how I set off the series of events that's landed both of us here.

I detest myself for what I've done.

"Don't bother," the trolless in the cage next to mine says. She has a stripe of short purple hair along the top of her head, and her skin is pale blue, like the sky. She has a huge round earring in one ear. "If he hasn't talked yet, he's not gonna."

The orc grunts. "He will eventually," he says. "Whether it's down here or in the arena, the king will make him talk. Or scream. Whichever comes first."

I wonder what this *arena* is that they're talking about. It must be why we're being kept here like exotic animals.

The two humans are having their own conversation, too, in Freysian. "Another trollkin, huh?" The big, muscled man with one eye, who sits in a cage near the entrance to our prison, chuckles darkly. "Guess I'll just have to chop off his head, too."

He assumes I can't understand him, being an ogre. There's no reason to rob him of that assumption, so I stay quiet.

"Good luck with that," says the older man, his body criss-crossed with scars. "That big oaf could probably kill any one of us with his bare hands. Look at the size of him."

"You're wrong, Fex. All you have to do with a guy like that is slash him behind the ankles. Once his legs give out... boom. He's helpless. Then you give him a knife through the throat."

I think I'm starting to understand. Whatever this arena is, we will likely have to fight each other in it. At least now I know how this big man will try to take me down.

But I can't take a knife to the throat while Mia still lives—while she's still waiting for me to find her and free her.

I shiver with rage at the thought of what that "king" might do with her. Where is she now? Is she safe? The not-knowing ties my stomach into painful knots. I examine the chain locking me down to the ground, wondering how difficult it might be to break.

The trolless chuckles as I weigh it in my hand. "Good fucking luck," she says, flopping down on the floor in her own cage. "Even if you broke that thing, how do you get out? There's nowhere to go, ogre."

Soon, everyone falls quiet again. There's an air of resignation in the room, as if the others have all given up any dream of escaping.

I will not fall to hopelessness, though. Perhaps if I can get out into this arena, without these chains holding me down, I have a chance at finding my Mia and getting out with her. I just have to survive long enough to do it.

CHAPTER 9

MIA

The revelers drink more and more as the night goes on. Fresh casks of mead and beer are rolled in, and mugs are refilled as people holler and shout at one another. The king observes it all with disinterest, his fingers tapping the arm of his chair.

I want to know what he's thinking—what he has planned for me when this festival of nonsense finally dies down, and why he took Cragnorr away. He's had a fair amount of booze himself, and I think I can weasel something out of him.

"You know," I say casually, leaning toward him in my chair, "it's quite a town you've built here."

He glances at me from the corner of his eye.

"I didn't build it," he says in a bored voice. "My daddy did."

"Where's he?" I ask.

"Dead." He maintains his deadpan expression as he reaches for his beer and slugs down some more.

That's not the answer I was hoping for.

"Oh?" I try to keep my tone light. "What happened to him?"

The King grins at me, revealing a full mouth of stained teeth. A few appear to be made of gold, or something that looks like it. If he weren't a bastard, he might be handsome under a flattering light. And if he didn't open his mouth.

"I killed him."

I gulp. Fuck, I shouldn't have started this conversation. I don't want to be discussing *killing* or *death* with this unhinged man.

"So, tell me," the King says, leaning on the arm of his chair to bring his head closer to mine. "Why is a pretty young girl wandering the woods with a trollkin?" He reeks, not just like booze but like he hasn't washed in a few weeks.

At least we're on the subject of Cragnorr now. Maybe I can find out what the King wants with him—and convince him that he won't get it.

"Perhaps she's fucking it," Gru interrupts, sipping his beer. "It was very protective of her when we found them."

The King looks at me with fresh surprise. "Oh? Is that so? Are you fucking the ogre?"

I splutter. "What?"

"Is his cock huge?" Gru asks. "How do you take it?"

I can't help thinking of Cragnorr in my hands, that thick length swelling in my grip. After that, I wondered the same question. Could I welcome that huge thing inside me?

It sends heat rolling through me, from my head to my toes.

A nasty chuckle brings my attention back to the King. "She *blushes*," he crows. "You might be right, Gru. If she's had ogre cock, what use does she have for human cock?"

The nasty, tiny man strokes his chin. "Perhaps she's not a good toy for you, sire. You should give her to me, instead."

A laugh bursts out of the King. "So you want her for yourself?" He grimaces. "An ugly creature like you?"

This clearly wounds Gru, who settles back into his chair with his arms crossed over his chest and falls silent, sipping on his mead like a kicked puppy.

So there's dissent here. That could be good.

"What do you want Cragnorr for, anyway?" I ask.

The King laughs at me. "Can't keep your mouth shut, can you? You'll find out soon enough."

The drinking continues, and soon, it's affecting the King, too. He lolls forward in his chair, then realizes what he's doing and quickly sits back up. He's forced a mug of beer in front of me, but when he realized that my arms were still tied to the chair, he took my beer for himself.

"All right!" he suddenly calls out, rising to his feet. He sways perilously. "I am off to bed! But please, put more logs on the fire and keep on."

Shouts ring out across the gathering, and the King is pleased with this answer. He has Gru untie me from the chair, then snatches the ropes up in his hand. He leans down so he's speaking right in my ear. "You're coming with me," he whispers.

The hairs on my neck stand up, and I resist the urge to cringe. But this could also be my moment. Everyone here is drunk as skunks, and even the King's grip on me is wavering.

So I nod agreeably, and the King smirks. "Good," he says, righting himself. "The less you fight, the better this will be for both of us."

Fuck. The better *what* will be?

He tugs on me to follow him, so I do obediently, hoping that maybe he'll drop his guard and I can break away. Behind the tent is a path lined with torches, leading to a small building that's just as crude as the other ones. Once we step out into the night, I glance around to see who else might be nearby, but everyone in the camp appears occupied with their party.

I have to think fast. We only have thirty, maybe forty more

steps to the door of the disjointed little cabin. I only wish I knew where they took Cragnorr. I can't leave without him.

"Whatever you're thinking," the King mumbles, yanking on my ropes to draw me closer to him, "you'll fail. And then you'll get an arrow through the heart for trying."

His warning kills any hope I might have had of making it out—tonight, at least. It might look like the camp is disorganized and chaotic, but whoever these people are, they're dangerous, too.

Still, I have to try. Maybe if I find out a little more about them and what they want, I can make a plan.

"Why does everyone call you the King?" I ask as we walk. "There's only one king."

His eyes flash with anger as we near the door. "I am the true king," he snarls, rounding on me. "And these are my chosen people. This land doesn't belong to *that* king. No, I am its ruler. I am its master. None of your pathetic laws matter here." He shoves the door of the little house open and pushes me inside. "Now stop your endless chatter."

At first it's quite dark, and I stand there trying to find my footing as the King reaches for something on the wall. After a few moments, a lamp is lit and hung up. Then he slams the door closed behind us, turning the lock.

My blood runs cold at that closed door. Now I'm trapped here, with him—with this filthy bastard who most definitely wants something from me, something I don't even want to think about.

I even my breathing and try not to panic. This man will seize on fear. Instead, I survey the room, which is far more opulent than I expected given the shoddy exterior.

But everything is almost... comically mismatched. There are pillows in all sorts of patterns arranged on the floor in a giant nest, covered in crumpled-up blankets. There's a dining table, piled high with gold and treasure and jewels. They glitter in the lamplight, just out in the open for anyone to see.

Clearly this "King" has plenty in the way of riches.

"Do you like it?" he asks, lighting another lamp near the pillows. My ropes now hang at my sides, but that doesn't mean anything. If I made a run for it, I'd have to stop at that door latch, and he'd easily be on top of me. "On our last raid, we came across a merchant. He was an old fuck, covered from head to toe in rubies." The King reaches a hand into the pile of jewels and lets them spill through his fingers like water. "Most of these rings wouldn't come off him, you know. I had to cut them off."

An involuntary shudder rolls down my spine, and he laughs at the look on my face. But the alcohol is starting its real work on him now, and when he tries to pick up one of his many jewels, he stumbles on one of the pillows behind him and falls back into his nest. He guffaws and holds out his arms to me.

"Come here, toy," he murmurs. Damn it, I need a way out of this. I have to convince this drunken idiot that he doesn't want me. "Come and give old Zake your pussy."

"Zake?" I ask, keeping my distance from him but using a soothing voice. "Is that your name?"

"Don't wear it out." His hands reach for me again, and horror washes over me as he pulls me down to the nest of pillows. I need a plan. I need to talk him out of doing this.

"I didn't answer your question before," I say as his hand slides down my side, over my hip and back up again. I try not to cringe, but all the hairs on my arms are standing on end.

"Which question?" His voice slurs.

"About whether I fucked the ogre or not."

Zake freezes. I lean in closer to him, trying to bear the stagnant stench. "I did," I whisper quietly. "I did fuck the ogre. I rode that big cock of his, and now I'll never, ever be tight again."

There. That should do it.

Fury crosses his face. Then he turns and spits on the floor.

"That's the most disgusting shit I've ever heard." He turns hard eyes on me. "A human, fucking a trollkin? An ogre, no less?" He looks like he's tasted something bad. "Get the fuck out of my bed."

I get up and dust myself off as Zake falls back into the nest, groaning.

"What a horrendous image," he mutters as I find a new spot on the floor to sit down. My nightgown does little to protect me. "Now it's burned into my mind."

"My apologies," I say, trying not to sound too self-satisfied.

I snag a pillow as I lie down, and already, Zake is snoring. I curl up in my nightgown, pulling my jacket close, and fall asleep remembering how wonderful it was to sleep in Cragnorr's arms.

CRAGNORR

Today will likely be my first fight, or so I've gathered from chatter among the other gladiators. That's what we are—warm bodies to be tossed into this *arena*, and made to battle to the death. That is why only half the cages are full: there's a constant cycle of residents coming and going as we're paired off.

Most of the time, only one combatant returns alive.

"It's nothing personal," the older man with the scars, Fex, tells me. "It's either kill or be killed, you know? We could be friends right now—" he lowers his eyebrows, "—not saying we are, but we could be. It wouldn't matter out there."

It didn't take long for them to realize I could understand what they're saying, even if I don't speak. I raised my head to pay attention to their conversations too many times, and now they include me, even as I try to sit and think instead.

"We're not friends," barks the big, hulking man farthest away from me, whose name I've gathered is Bino. "None of us are. And I won't hesitate to kill any one of you if it means I get out of here."

I sit forward in the cage at this, wincing when the collar bites into my neck. There's a way out of here if I win?

Bino laughs at me. "That sort of thing isn't for you, ogre," he says. "Humans like me, maybe we can leave once we've served our time. But not trollkin. You're as good as dead. That 'King' fellow will cycle you in and out until you finally lose."

Still, I cling to that shred of hope. Perhaps I can convince the bandit king that I am not one of them, that I can speak the human language and know their customs, and I deserve my freedom, too.

"Fresh blood always goes first," Fex says. "He wants to test ya. Find out what makes you tick. Which only matters if you can survive your first fight, of course."

We don't know who will fight until the stout woman with the baton comes for us, I gather. When she finally does arrive, I'm not surprised to see her walk toward my cage. The guards unhook my chain and then open the door, six of them crowded around in case I try to make a run for it. Instead, I'm perfectly obedient as they lead me out of the metal bars, to the other side of the room.

I realize it's not a wall, but a huge wooden door. Behind me, the other guards open Bino's cage.

"Are you fuckin' serious?" he demands as they chain him up by the wrists. "You're gonna make me fight the ogre?"

The woman with the baton scoffs. "Shouldn't be a problem for you, should it, big shot?"

Bino raises a fist, but one of the guards jerks him roughly by the chains. Though his head only reaches to my shoulder, I'm not so arrogant as to think he'll be easy to take down. No, this man is a brute, and he will stop at nothing to kill me and save his own hide. I remember how he talked about slashing my ankles, and I'll make sure in our fight not to expose any vulnerable areas to him.

As cheers swell outside the door, the guards present each of us with a weapon. Bino receives a massive axe, and I'm given a sword.

For a human it would be a short sword, but for me, it's a dagger. And I know what I'm intended to use it for.

The roar of some distant crowd grows louder until suddenly, the guards kick down the door. It lands on the dirt with a *boom*, splashing us in bright sunlight, and a cacophony of cheering envelopes me. I have to cover my ears just to keep my head from falling off my shoulders.

Now I know what this *arena* is. We are in a massive, circular pit carved out of the earth. The walls rise high around us, so high there's no possible way I could climb out. People are gathered up above us, hundreds of them, all shouting and screaming.

I scan the assembled people, wondering if Mia is among them. She doesn't know most of the things I've done in my life. She doesn't know that I've fought wolves with my bare hands. She doesn't know about the bear who once caught me off-guard at the lake, and I had to break his neck before he would let me go.

Now she'll see what a brute I truly am.

Finally, my eyes land on her. Above the crowd is a raised wooden platform, where I find that man, the 'King'—with my Mia sitting next to him, bound to a chair by rope.

My heart sinks like a stone. What has he done to her in the night we've been apart? Mia looks surprised when she sees me walk out into the arena, and she tries to get up, but her bindings keep her down.

"Cragnorr!" she calls. "Cragnorr!"

Her face is etched with worry, and I wish I could tell her there's no reason to worry. I would never let someone take me from her.

<h1 style="text-align:center">Chapter 10</h1>

Mia

"I told you that you'd enjoy today's match," Zake says in an irritating, satisfied tone. He slings an arm around the back of my chair and leans toward me. "Now you get to watch your ogre die."

I didn't want to believe it when Cragnorr stepped out of the dark tunnel inside the pit. The king had hidden what I could expect today, merely telling me I would have quite a lot of fun.

I knew then I wouldn't like whatever he had planned. And sure enough, it's the worst thing I could imagine.

That other guy looks mean and dangerous. Maybe it's the way he holds himself like this is just another day, or how he casually carries an axe slung over his shoulder... but I'm afraid of him.

And I'm terrified of what he'll do to my ogre.

"Cragnorr!" I holler. I don't know what I plan to do or say, but I need to see him, to talk to him, to do anything in my power to stop this from happening. He pauses in the middle of the arena and gazes up at me with a forlorn look. Then, to my surprise, his eyebrows lower in determination.

He's trying to tell me that he'll win. I want to believe it, but this other guy...

Cragnorr and the burly man find their way to opposite sides of the pit. They circle each other, the man dragging his axe in the dirt and drawing a long line behind him. Cragnorr palms the hilt of his sword. He may look like a lumbering giant, but I get the sense now that's only a part of him. When he whirls on the other man he looks fearsome, his big lower jaw jutting out, his huge tusks shining in the sun.

"You think you're tough?" the bear of a man asks, lifting his axe. "Wait until I cut off one of your arms."

My very skin shivers. Cragnorr isn't a fighter. At least he has a weapon, but... I can't stand the idea that this might be the last time I see him.

I have to stop this.

"Zake," I hiss. "This isn't going to be the fight you want it to be. Cragnorr's not a killer."

But the asshole only grins at me. "If he wasn't one before, he'll become one today." He shrugs. "Or he'll die."

I curl my hands into fists, wishing I could just smack that look right off his face, but I don't want to get my own head cut off.

"You don't have faith in him?" Zake asks, picking a ripe berry from a platter next to him. "That's sad. You'll take his cock but you won't back him in a fight?"

It's not that I don't have faith in him—it's that I don't want to see my sweet, peaceful ogre corrupted by violence. I don't want him to have to change just to survive.

I look down over the arena as Cragnorr and the bear-man circle each other, neither wanting to take the first step. I can't watch, but I have to.

For him.

CRAGNORR

Bino snickers as we both pad around the edge of the arena. "Come on now," he calls to me, beckoning. "Attack me, won't you, big guy? I don't want to have to come over there."

I ignore him, keeping one eye on the platform overhead where Mia is being kept prisoner. She's watching me with huge eyes, hands clenched into fists. There has to be an answer to all of this, a way out of here that doesn't involve butchering.

I test the sword in my hand. It's heavier than my hunting knife, but much sharper and deadlier. Wielding it shouldn't present a problem, but humans are smarter than animals, and those are the only opponents I've faced before today.

Finally, tired of waiting, Bino leans forward and bolts across the arena toward me. He reels his axe back over his head, ready to deliver a powerful strike.

But he doesn't move nearly as fast as I expected, and the trajectory of his weapon is clear enough from the positioning of his body. I take a single step to the side and he blows past me, hurling his axe into the dirt. Two more steps forward and now I'm along his flank, my sword raised.

I can't shed blood in front of Mia. And I couldn't live with myself if I killed this man just for this crowd's entertainment.

So I aim my pommel and strike him with it in the back. He howls, stumbling forward.

"Damn ogre!" Bino roars, turning around to face me. His skin is red all over now—I've made him angry.

He charges again, and this time I raise my sword to meet the huge blade of his axe, gambling that I can best him in strength. Our weapons meet in a terrible clash of metal that bounces around the inside of my head. Luckily, I'm much bigger than Bino is, so as I press forward using my weapon like a baton, he slides backwards across the dirt, unable to overcome me.

I think of what he said about slashing someone's ankles as a way to bring them down for good. Abruptly I release the pressure on my sword. With Bino's full body weight leaned into his axe, the moment I pull away, he loses his balance and stumbles toward me. He extends one foot to catch himself, so I sweep my leg out and slam it into his shin as hard as I can.

"Fuck!" Bino shouts as he tumbles to the ground on his belly, his axe skidding away. I jump on him, slamming one foot down into the center of his back. He shrieks in pain, but I made sure not to hit him so hard that I broke anything.

Now he's trapped underneath me, with no way to escape.

"Kill him!" a shout rises from the assembled humans overhead.

"Kill him!" calls out someone else.

Soon the cries are all unified: *Kill him, kill him, kill him!* They're frantic, desperate for bloodletting. I look down at Bino, who now lies facedown in the dust.

"Get it over with!" he growls, turning his head so he can glare up at me with one eye. "End it already!"

Instead, I drop my sword to the ground with a metallic *clank*.

The air fills with the roar of everyone booing. The crowd is jeering at me, infuriated that they're losing their bloodshed as I refuse to cut off Bino's head.

"Fucking end it!" Bino hollers from his place trapped under my foot. But I'm not going to play the King's game. I pull my foot off of him, and then pick up his axe. Without hesitating, I fling it against the nearest wall, where it buries itself in the dirt ten feet up. Now someone would have to be my size to reach it and pull it out.

Grunting with effort, the human man drags himself back up to his feet. His face is filled with rage.

"Are you trying to humiliate me?" he demands, stalking toward me. He has no weapon now, but that doesn't seem to faze him. He lunges, wielding only his bare hands, and tries to wrap his fingers around my thick throat. But he's slow, unfocused, and I think injured, so it's easy to block him and throw him to the ground again.

Bino gags as all the wind is knocked out of his lungs. I need to put him down—enough for this fight to be over. So I lift my foot, aim for his chest, and slam it into him. He gasps and his eyes fly wide, then he curls up in a ball on the ground.

He's not getting up anytime soon. The crowd roars even more angrily as I toss my sword away.

No one will be dying today.

MIA

"Damn it!" Zake slams his fist into the arm of his chair. "This is not what I got my hands on a fucking *ogre* for."

Why did he do it? Why did Cragnorr let that man live? He'll simply have to fight another day, and maybe next time, Cragnorr won't be so lucky as to face off against such a simple-minded opponent.

My ogre with his soft heart. I don't know what I'll do with him.

Cragnorr's soon seized by guards and led away, back into the dark cavern where he came from, the other man limping along behind. Then the door is closed once more as the crowd empties out, most of them grumbling. When we leave, Zake drags me along behind him as if I'm little more than an annoying dog.

"That bastard," Zake growls when he finds his way into the tent to find the tables stacked with food. He sits down at the head, but this time, there's no chair for me. He points at the floor. "As long as your boyfriend doesn't perform for me, you'll get the scraps." To make his point, he tosses an apple onto the floor at me, and it rolls until it bumps into my knee. But all I can think about is what they must be doing down there to Cragnorr to punish him for today.

"What are you going to do with him if he won't fight?" I ask from my spot on the ground. I shift as the ropes bite into my wrists. Now my nightgown is filthier than ever. "You can't make him raise a sword. You should just let him go."

He barks a condescending laugh. "Oh, don't worry. I'll find a way to make him draw blood." He grins down at me with those yellowed teeth of his, and a gold cap glints in the light. "There's a key for every lock." With a wink, he takes a big swig of his beer, and slams the mug down on the table.

While the King devours his meal, I take stock of the camp. The big pit where the gladiators fought today appears to be at the center, which will certainly make everything more difficult. The high walls protecting the perimeter end where the hillside begins, and I wonder how hard it would be to climb. Cragnorr is excellent at climbing, and though the rock face looks steep from here, I think together we could scale it.

Maybe that's our ticket out of here, if I can manage to get to Cragnorr. He's being kept somewhere underneath the ground, near the arena. I just have to figure out how to get inside.

"Hungry?" the King asks, tossing me a rib bone that still has some meat left on it. But my hands are still bound, so I just glare up at him. He laughs.

"It's not too late to give her to me," Gru says. The tall woman with the braid sits on the other side of him, and gives him a disgusted look.

"So now you want to fuck the ogre's slut?" she says, breaking a bone in half and sucking out the marrow. She glances at the King. "What are you going to do with her, Your Majesty?"

He frowns down at me, and I wish she hadn't asked. Sitting on the floor is the least of my worries.

"I don't know. She doesn't do me much good now." He cocks his head. "I wonder how long it takes for the stench of ogre to come off?"

"Never," I say from my position on the ground.

The woman with the braid chuckles. "Good luck breaking this one," she says. "Why bother, Zake? Like you said, she's not queen material."

He *hmph*s. "She'll make a good toy once that ogre is dead." A smile spreads across his face. "And we can arrange that soon enough."

A heavy stone of foreboding settles in my stomach. Cragnorr walking away from that fight only put him in a worse position. Now the King is going to find a way to *make* him fight, and he might not survive it this time.

The woman with the braid stands up from the table and, tucking her hands behind her, pads over to where I'm seated on the floor.

"She's filthy," she says, surveying me. "Let me take her for the night, Your Majesty, and after tomorrow's fight, she'll be in prime condition for your claiming."

Claiming? "Nobody's claiming me," I say, pulling away, which only ends up with me flopping over on my side like a fish.

Zake's eyes brighten at this as they all ignore me. "A purifying?" he asks. "Perfect. Exactly what she needs."

The woman grabs my arm and hauls me up to my feet, then jerks on the rope tying my wrists together. "Come with me, little slut," she says in a sing-song voice, like she's trying to convince an animal to follow her across a river.

Maybe this is good luck. I'm going to be separated from Zake for the night, and maybe I'll learn more about the camp—something that could help us escape this place. It sounds like tomorrow might be Cragnorr's last chance.

I have to save him before that happens.

CRAGNORR

After the fight, I was thrown into my cage with careless abandon, the guards infuriated at me for ruining their fun. At least tonight I won't have to sleep with the metal collar around my neck, because they forgot to clip me down before stomping away.

That night, I'm given some bones that have already been mostly picked over and little else. "Fucker," Bino growls at me when he's also given nothing but a few pieces of rotted food, in exchange for losing—and surviving it. "I'm going to kill you next time we fight. Hell, maybe before then."

I don't answer, of course. We are all victims, and I refuse to participate in the King's games. Especially not with Mia watching.

"You can try," says Fex with a snort. "But we all got a good look at the fight, and you were slow and sloppy. The ogre had you on the ropes."

Bino glares daggers at Fex, but doesn't speak more as he tries to pick out the good parts of his food.

"Trying to impress your woman?" the trolless next to me asks in Trollkin. She's been watching me for some time, like she's sizing me up. "With that show out there?"

I cock my head. She knows about Mia?

"It was obvious to everyone. You care about the woman that detestable leader of theirs has his claws in." She examines her nails. "You can speak the human language, so it makes sense."

When I don't answer, she sighs and leans back against the bars of her cage. "I'm Pa'zi, by the way."

I nod.

"Not going to tell me yours, huh, big guy?"

She doesn't need to know my name. No one needs to know anything about me before I can get out of here.

"Are you fucking her?" the orc asks, stepping to the front of his cage to get in on the conversation. "The little human?"

I don't know what this *fucking* means. I give him a blank look.

"You know," the orc says, rolling his eyes. He holds up a circle with one hand, and mimes sticking another finger through it. "Putting your cock in her."

I glance down at my groin, trying to imagine what he means by this. Is the circle meant to represent her mouth? I did consider such a thing after I feasted on Mia between the legs. If her hands felt that good around me, I wondered what her mouth would feel like. Is that what he means?

At my quizzical look, the orc shakes his head. "No way," he says to Pa'zi. "I don't think our ogre here knows what his cock is for."

She snorts. "Is that right?" Hands wrapped around the bars, she presses her face through it, grinning mischievously at me. "Do you know what a cunt is, big guy?"

Again, I'm at a loss. Her smile only widens. She reaches down between her legs and drags a hand through them. I stare as she touches it again. She must have one of those soft, wet holes there, too. Then she holds up a circle, like the orc did.

"A cunt," she explains, winking at me. "Have you ever seen one?"

So that is what she means. I nod. I've seen the most beautiful cunt in the entire world. I licked it and sucked on it and put my fingers inside it to make Mia cry out with her pleasure.

"Ah." Pa'zi hums. "So he's seen a cunt, but never put his cock in one."

I blink. Cocks go inside… cunts?

A sudden, powerful heat takes over my body when I imagine my cock fitting into that hot channel at the crux of Mia's thighs. The damn thing immediately answers, rising under my trousers. How would it even fit?

But oh, if it did, I would be the luckiest ogre in all of history.

"I bet you saw that human's cunt, didn't you?" says Pa'zi, smirking.

"Ha!" The orc pats his belly as he chuckles. "So she let you see it, but wouldn't let you fuck it?"

The question didn't even come up. I wonder if Mia knows about this cocks-inside-cunts business. I know it would feel marvelous for me—would it do the same for her? Would she moan like she did when I pumped my finger inside her?

"What a tease," says Pa'zi. "You didn't even get to fuck a cunt before you died? Tragic."

"He was probably too big for her." The orc snorts. "No way that pole of a cock could fit."

"Guess we'll never know."

They're wrong, though. I won't die here. I won't die as long as Mia is in the King's captivity. I will get her out of here, if it's the last thing I do. And it might very well be.

Then I would die knowing I lived my purpose.

MIA

I follow along behind the woman with the big, swinging braid as she leads me away from the tent, off to another part of the camp that's not nearly as well-lit. We stop at a water pump surrounded by buckets.

"Get filling," she says, kicking a bucket towards me. I've seen this woman in action before, so I don't hesitate to comply, putting the bucket under the faucet and pumping the handle to bring up water. When it's filled, she waves a hand at me to follow her. I carry the huge, heavy bucket along behind her to a rather large wooden tub, where she instructs me to pour it in.

Then I fill another bucket, and another, until the tub is halfway full.

"Now get in," she tells me. A bath? It might be frigid cold, but don't mind if I do.

I strip off my clothes, glancing around once to see who's watching, but we're alone. Then I climb into the tub full of frigid water. The evening is cool but not chilly, and soon I adjust to the temperature of the water.

"Wash up good," the woman says, taking her hair out of her braids to brush it while I bathe. "Don't want any of that ogre stink when the King makes his decision about what to do with you."

My stomach does a flip, and I feel sick. Right. She's "purifying" me.

The camp is significantly quieter here, with no homes in the immediate area, just crates of storage and piles of junk. This place must be reserved for bathing, an activity which people here don't seem too keen on.

I take it all in, wondering if this might be the way out of here. It doesn't even look like there are guards on the nearby pike wall.

The woman hands me a bar of soap, which I use to scrub

myself all over, including my thick, long hair. She watches me as I dunk under the water and rinse it out.

"I'm Narria," she tells me at last. "And you should be very grateful to me."

I sit up in the tub. "Why's that?" I ask. "Why should I be grateful to someone keeping me captive, who plans to hand me over like a piece of meat? Who's keeping my friend and forcing him to fight?"

"Friend, huh?" She arches an eyebrow. "Been spinning a little lie, have you?"

Fuck. Me and my stupid mouth. Maybe I haven't taken Crag-norr's cock *there*, but I've done plenty of other things with him. Calling him a 'friend' doesn't feel quite honest, but I'm not sure what other word to use.

My shoulders tense. "You do what you have to do," I answer, hoping she won't turn me in to Zake right away for my fib. "I'm just trying to survive."

She doesn't answer. No, Narria surveys me while I finish bathing, not speaking. When I'm done rinsing my hair, I get out of the tub and shiver in the cool night air as the water evaporates off of me. With a sigh, Narria grabs a span of fabric and hands it to me.

"Dry off," she says, so I do obediently. When I reach for my nightgown and jacket, though, she stops me. She chucks them away into the pile of abandoned objects nearby, and I watch my filthy nightgown go with a smidgen of remorse. That was the last vestige of my old life.

Peering into a big basket of other clothing items, Narria picks through it until she finds what she's looking for. She presents me with a long tunic and a pair of soft leggings, and insists I put them on.

"There. Fit for a King." She laughs at her own joke. "Now come on. Better get you rested up for tomorrow."

"What's tomorrow?" I ask as she reties the rope around my wrists.

"You'll see." She tugs on the ropes, and I follow her back to the main area of the camp. She opens the flap to a particularly big tent, and inside I find a platform bed, racks of weapons, and a few chairs assembled around a quaint fire pit.

"We'll have to share tonight," she tells me, closing the tent flap and tying it. Then she pats the blankets, and I sit down. Narria ties my rope around the leg of the bed so I can't try to escape in the middle of the night, but makes sure to leave plenty of slack so I can still lie down comfortably.

She's been surprisingly nice to me. I'm clean and dressed, and I'm going to sleep in a warm bed tonight, too. If I just pretend she doesn't plan to hand me over to Zake tomorrow, I could almost enjoy it.

"Why are you doing this?" I ask as I lie down. Narria stoops by the fire pit to light it.

"Doing what?" After piling up dry pine needles under some logs, she clicks a fire starter and the twigs catch.

"Keeping me away from Zake tonight," I say. She didn't need to be kind to me. It's almost like she was doing me a favor by delaying my fate another day.

Narria pauses, then turns around to face me. "I know what he wants with you." She sets her jaw. "And I wouldn't wish it on my worst enemy. I figure the least I can do is give you one last good night before he steals your innocence."

I blink at her. How does she know I'm a virgin?

"It's obvious," she says, answering my question for me. "You wouldn't have called the ogre your 'friend' if you weren't." She blows on the flames to urge them higher. "The King will get tired of you soon enough, though. You'll be different afterwards, but at least he'll let you go when he gets his hands on a new toy."

I shudder all over. So he'll use me until he finds someone else. I should be happy to learn this, that someday I'll be free of him—but how long will it take for him to get bored of me? And what will I have to bear in the meantime?

Then it occurs to me why she's telling me this, and why she's helping me.

"Did you used to belong to him?" I ask. Narria's shoulders tense up in front of the fire, and that's all the answer I need.

After a few moments of silence, she stands up and walks over to the bed, climbing over me to get to the other side. She pulls the blankets up over us, and we both stare up at the roof of the tent where a hole lets the smoke escape.

"I lasted for about two months," Narria finally says. "I was much more willing than you, though. I didn't have anyone else, and being the center of Zake's attention was like a drug. He has a lot of power, and I thought he would share that power with me. I thought he'd make me his Queen."

I turn to face her, but Narria's eyes are closed as she speaks.

"He had no intention of doing that, of course. We're just playthings to him. He's looking for someone to warm up his bed and that's all."

I shiver involuntarily. And I'm next on the docket.

"So enjoy your last night without some greasy asshole putting his cock in you." She pats my arm, and then rolls over, indicating it's time for bed now.

"What about Cragnorr?" I ask, and Narria shifts to glance over her shoulder at me. "What's... what's going to happen to him?"

"Well, the ogre's going to die," she says, as if this is the most obvious thing in the world. "You didn't know that?"

I've been holding off the tears for some time now, but at this simple declaration, they finally spring free.

My ogre. My best friend.

I have to get him out of here before that happens. I'll do anything.

Narria sighs in annoyance. "You care too much," she says, turning away from me again. "But that'll get ripped out of you soon enough."

She falls asleep quickly, and is soon snoring next to me. But I lie awake for what feels like hours, picturing Cragnorr's gruff face, with his long tusks and brutish brows. I can almost feel his big body against mine, holding me tight as we slept on the forest floor.

Tomorrow, I have one choice if I'm going to free him and make that future possible. It will break his heart, but it's the only way he'll survive.

When I manage to drift off, it's by imagining that we're together again.

CHAPTER 12

CRAGNORR

After the others fall asleep that night, I stay awake with the bars of my cage biting into my back. The scrape of the metal makes me remember I'm still alive, that I have choices, that I have power.

I wonder what's happening to Mia up there, under the King's thumb, and hope against hope that he hasn't hurt her. I think of her sweet, small body resting in my arms, and my bastard of a dick lifts its head up. Now that the idea of sliding myself into her has been put in my mind, I can't unlearn it. My blood pulses as I think of how she might feel inside that cavern between her thighs.

My body is too hot and my mind is too preoccupied for sleep. I'm filled with just as much anxiety as lust, and it's all painfully confusing. I try to sort through it, to put these images of Mia's round breasts and curved hips out of my head, but they keep returning. So I turn my back to the others, untie my pants, bring out my warm cock, and squeeze it hard thinking of her.

My human. My everything. What I wouldn't give to be with her again, to listen to her soft sighs as she sleeps, to taste her beautiful cunt. I'd bring her in close and nuzzle her hair, inhaling her perfect smell, keeping her safe from everything in the world that might try to hurt her.

I stroke myself harder and harder, keeping as silent as I can, imagining how she tastes. I wonder if my cock would even fit if I put it there. Just thinking about this, imagining her underneath me, I erupt—but I make sure to spill outside of the cage.

What if I was too big for her? I look down at my limp cock, furrowing my brow. Maybe I'm not meant to have her, and that's why I'm here in this dungeon. Maybe this is all a punishment for thinking I'm worthy of Mia's body and heart.

Am I an idiot for believing that I could be hers? That the world would allow us to be together?

Thoroughly exhausted, I slide down onto the floor and don't even dream.

The next morning, the guards bring us food—and I'm rather surprised to find a massive platter in front of me, heaped with sausage and bread, cooked greens and fruit, and even what looks like a piece of pie. Every single head in the room turns.

"What the fuck?" demands Bino. "This asshole won't even fight and he's getting treated like royalty?"

Fex shakes his head with a sigh. "It's a last meal," he explains to me. "The King expects you to die today, but he wants you to put on a good show first. The food is so you have plenty of energy out there to put up a fight."

Oh. That, unfortunately, makes a lot of sense. I wonder what he has planned. If I can survive whatever that bastard throws at me today, perhaps replenishing my food stores could help. They left me unchained last night out of forgetfulness. The bars of my cage are strong, but I might be stronger if I were sufficiently fed.

A few hours later, the guards come for me. They clip a chain to my collar and shackle me, then lead me to the big wooden door that opens into the arena. I try to breathe, because there's no way for me to know what waits on the other side. My best option is to calm myself and be prepared for anything.

Boom! They kick down the door and lead me out into the pit. My bindings are removed, and then I'm alone. I glance around, waiting for someone else to arrive, but there's no one except me here.

My eyes jump up to the raised platform, and I spot Mia immediately.

Not only is she not tied up, but she's sitting in the king's lap as if she has always been there.

It can't be. Not my Mia. My eyes focus and unfocus again as I watch her seated up there, scooping a berry off a platter and feeding it right into his mouth. My heart thuds hard and fast, as if it's about to burst out of my chest.

Even worse, she looks... different. She's dressed in clothing that highlights her figure—a scrap of fabric covered in shiny silver scales barely holds her breasts in place, and her long, dark hair is clean and shining. More silver fabric covers her cunt, but little else.

That can't be her, my human girl, crawling all over some monster. My breathing speeds up as I watch, as I take in the way she feeds another berry into that disgusting man's mouth. She's *smiling*.

That is what drives a knife deep into my gut. Is she truly happier there, with him?

She has food, clothing, and likely a warm place to sleep. It's far more than I could ever offer her, in here or outside. Of course she would be brighter, more alive, with proper care.

Perhaps all my worst imaginings were wrong. Perhaps this

place is better for her. What if that foul human cares for her, and she cares for him in return?

Has she forgotten me so easily?

I knew a human would be a better match for her, that she would be safer among her own kind. The mere thought crushes me, grinding me into dust. What we shared was special, but not forever. It was a brief glimpse into a life I could never have, that I've known from the beginning was never meant for me.

Then I hear it—a growl, deep and rumbling. My eyes are drawn to the other wooden door on the opposite end of the arena. The growl erupts in a roar, and the wood shakes as something behind it tries to get out.

Whatever is back there is big, and it's dangerous.

The door is kicked down, and then my opponent is revealed: a massive lion, but it's unlike any of the mountain lions I've seen, standing nearly twice as tall with light stripes down its sides, and a strange mane down its back. It must be some sort of hybrid—and it's truly a monster.

The lion-creature steps out into the arena, already enraged by whatever they were doing to it behind the door. I have a vision of those huge, scythe-like claws cutting my flesh into ribbons.

The crowd goes absolutely wild, cheering and screaming. The lion is further irritated by this, and swings its head before charging me.

In its fury, it rushes me blindly, and I manage to side-step the swipe of its gargantuan paw. But my eyes are drawn again to where Mia sits atop the king's lap, his arms casually curled around her.

Surely I'm seeing things. This isn't real. This can't truly be my Mia. She would never give herself over to him, would she? There must be a reason behind this, behind why everything has changed overnight.

Another horrible roar reminds me where I am, and I barely

dodge another swipe. I have to be here, and focus on the now if I'm going to make it through this fight. Then I will find out the truth.

My avoidance tactics are making the lion-hybrid even angrier. It rises up onto two legs and lunges at me, swinging its huge paws in wide arcs, one after another. I duck, then side-step, and duck again. I have to put some distance between us, because eventually one will hit.

But on my next step, I don't leap back far enough to get out of the way. I take a massive blow to the chest, the lion's claws digging into my flesh and tearing some out as it withdraws. I stumble, gasping as I try to bring breath back into my lungs. This time when the lion roars, it's so close that spittle showers my face.

Good. It's just close enough.

I curl my hand into a fist and punch as hard as I can, throwing my entire body weight behind it. I sock the huge animal square in the head, and it howls. For a moment, the lion is distracted by my attack, and I use the opportunity to run. I need a better plan than punching lions in the head.

When I reach the other side of the pit, my eyes travel up again to Mia. She's leaned back, whispering something in the king's ear. My entire body heats, filling up my head with a new, painful feeling, something I've never encountered before.

Jealousy, hatred for this man whose hands are all over her.

Was I wrong all along about us and what we mean to each other?

Mia

I'm so close to getting him to listen. All I want is for Zake to give Cragnorr a sword, or an axe—anything he can use to defend himself. Narria has dressed me in the prettiest, skimpiest clothes she could find to give me as good of a chance as possible of seducing Zake into saving Cragnorr's life.

"The lion has such sharp claws," I whisper in his ear. "The ogre should have something sharp, too. It will be a much better fight." Since I was cleaned up and presented to him by Narria this morning, the king has taken a much deeper interest in me. He told me that if I sat in his lap, I could watch the match without ropes holding me down.

If I have to strangle him with my bare hands, I will. But a sharp object would be a lot easier. I just have to find the right opportunity. Maybe I'll be killed or hanged or something worse when I figure out a way to kill Zake, but I have no choice.

None of this will end until he's gone.

"But your ogre has a brain," Zake points out. "The lion is just an animal. Surely he can best it with those big fists of his."

I shake my head and feed the King another berry, glancing back at the fight whenever possible. Cragnorr is on the run, and my heart is racing in my chest even as I try to play calm and coy in Zake's lap.

"You want to create a butcher, don't you?" I ask. "Cragnorr could be your prize fighter. Put the taste of blood in his mouth by letting him kill the lion with a sword, and he'll be changed."

The king chews, thinking this over.

"Fine," he says at last. He sets me down on the ground, and I'm grateful for this moment of respite. I've felt like throwing up all over him since we arrived and he put his hands on me. Even worse was feeling his cock under his pants as I sat on his lap.

Zake removes a hand axe from his hip, then rises to his feet and holds it high up over his head. "A gift!" he calls out to Cragnorr. He reels his arm back, then throws it down into the ring. The axe buries itself in the dirt a few yards away. "From your whore!"

Cragnorr's eyes leap up to the platform, and he scowls deeply.

I've never seen such rage in his eyes, and it cuts into a part of my heart I didn't know I had.

I know I've hurt him today, probably irreparably. But it's what I had to do to keep him alive.

And yet, he doesn't go for the axe. He circles the lion as it spins around again and charges toward him. At this point he's going to run out of energy, and then the lion will land another hit that could be lethal. Already Cragnorr is bleeding from the chest where it got through his defenses—but still, he doesn't pick up the axe.

Why? Why won't he protect himself?

It goes on like this, with Cragnorr and the lion circling one another, and Cragnorr dodging every one of its attacks. Zake grows more and more tense underneath me. He's angry that Cragnorr hasn't taken his offering, and that bodes poorly for both of us.

Once more the lion swipes at my ogre, and once more he steps out of the way. People are booing and jeering, and they even start throwing food into the arena.

"I'm done with this." Zake abruptly stands up, sending me sprawling. He waves at Narria and Gru, who both stand nearby. "Put her in."

Narria blinks as I get back to my feet. "Her, Your Majesty?" she asks, eyes darting over to me and back. "With the liger?"

"It's obvious, fools," he growls as Gru grabs my wrists. There's no point trying to get away from him, not now. Cragnorr has sealed my fate. "The ogre only cares about her. He won't fight unless I *make him*."

Zake whistles, earning the attention of the crowd. But I already know what he's going to say.

He's going to force Cragnorr to fight, with me as the bait.

"Let's raise the stakes, shall we?" he calls out. The crowd murmurs, listening. Gru drags me to my feet and leads me to a platform that hangs over the arena. I dig in my heels and yank backward.

"No!" I can't go out like this, not before I take Zake with me. Down there, in the pit, I can't possibly help Cragnorr. I'll only get in the way. "Don't do this. I can ask him to fight and he will. I promise!"

Zake yawns dramatically, and urges Gru onward. I find Narria's gaze as I go, but she just shakes her head sadly. Gru and two others grab me by the arms and shove me forward, over the edge of the pit.

"And now," Zake calls out as I fall, "the damsel in distress arrives!"

CHAPTER 13

My blood is hammering in my ears as they drag Mia off the platform and, in one push, shove her over the wall.

No. Not my Mia. She can't be down here with me, with this monster. Perhaps it was horrible to see her in the King's lap, but it's even worse to see her sentenced to the same fate that I am.

She tumbles down and lands on her side, letting out a terrible cry of pain. The lion is just as distracted as I am by this new arrival. When Mia moans in agony, the lion pivots towards her, drawn by her cries. Then it careens away from me faster than I can track.

Fuck. I can't let it get anywhere near her with fangs and claws like those.

I charge after it at full speed. Though the lion is fast, my woman is lying on the ground on the other side of the arena, and a fresh heat is pumping through my blood that grants me new strength and speed.

I throw my whole body at the big animal, slamming into its hip with my shoulder. The lion stumbles to one side, away from the impact. It skids, then spins around so we're facing each other.

I glance at Mia from the corner of my eye. She's trying to stand up, and I don't think anything is broken.

The lion advances on me, but I can't play this game anymore, not with Mia in the ring with us. I have to end the fight immediately if I want to keep her safe.

"Cragnorr!" she calls out. "The axe!"

Her voice attracts the lion's attention, just long enough for me to run toward the axe where the blade is buried in the ground. When I sweep it up into my hand, the assembled crowd cheers and howls. The lion is stalking toward Mia, and she backs away until she's pushed up against the wall of the pit.

I have one job. There is a single reason why I was born into this world, and it's to protect her. I will be her guardian from now until the day I die, which might be today.

"Beast!" I shout, stomping one foot so hard the ground shivers. The lion-monster turns its head, regarding me. My vision is honing in on my enemy, and the air shimmers with red. I will kill it before it touches a single hair on her head. I will kill anyone and anything for Mia.

I charge. The lion raises a paw to bat me away, but I'm swinging with the axe at the same time, and I bury it in the lion's front leg. Rearing back, it lets out an ear-piercing roar.

Now it's exposed to me. My blood is rushing fast, making all of my limbs taut and strong. I'm consumed by only one need: to kill. To destroy. To protect my Mia from anything that would try to hurt her.

I will erase any obstacle in my path.

I raise the axe high up over my head and, with a bellow, I slash down with all the might in my body. It slices the lion clean through, from throat to chest.

Blood spurts out, and this time the lion's cry is a shriek. Gasps rise up from the audience as I cut across again, making sure to tear through its throat. With one last terrible burble of blood, the huge body crumples to the ground with a *thump*.

I'm panting hard, hot fury filling every one of my veins. When I'm certain that the lion is no longer breathing, I stalk over toward where Mia is staring at me, eyes wide in horror. But I don't care how she sees me. I care only about her, right here in front of me, in all of her perfect beauty. The rage pulses inside me, twisting and curling into something else. Everything is driving me towards her —tangling my hands in her long hair, wrapping her up in me.

I grab Mia, seizing her whole body in my arms, and crush her to my chest. She squeaks, but I don't let her go. I hold her there, breathing in the smell of her, knowing that she is safe.

But I have ignored the world around us for too long. The King is now on his feet, shouting an order.

"Drop them!" he calls. Then, quite suddenly, there's nothing underneath us.

When the trap door opens, we tumble straight down into it. I twist my body in the air to cushion Mia's fall, and my back connects with something impossibly hard. It sends a ripple of pain through my body, and I grit my teeth—but the bloodlust still filling me absorbs it. I manage to land with Mia on top of me, but now she's spilled out of my arms onto the floor.

Overhead, the trap door closes again, leaving us in near-total darkness, only a strip of light shining down between the doors.

I roar in fury, trying to reach out and push them open again, but it's far too high up.

"Cragnorr?" Mia says in a small voice. Behind me, she's getting back up to her feet and once again my eyes hone in on her.

Mia. My Mia.

The power flowing through my body redirects into one purpose: making her mine.

MIA

In all the years I've known Cragnorr, which is almost his entire life, I've never seen him like this. His teeth are gritted and his brows are furrowed, his nostrils flaring with every labored breath. His eyes are wild, pupils blown-out and gigantic, and his fingers are clenched into stiff claws. Even his muscles look bigger, all swelled up with blood.

That's not the only place it's gone. Under his pants, his cock is thick, pressing hard at the fabric of his dirty pants.

He takes a step towards me, and if it were anyone but Cragnorr, I would back away, and perhaps try to hide. There would be nowhere to go in this little dark, underground room. The one metal door is heavy and locked.

"Mia," he says, and I'm so unused to hearing his voice that I freeze. "My Mia."

In one swift, rough motion, Cragnorr grabs me and wraps me tightly in his arms. His hands cover every part of me, my back, my hips, my ass. His hot breath hits my ear as he lowers his head and brushes my cheek with his tusk.

"Cragnorr?" I ask, unsure what's come over him. He rubs his nose against my throat and groans in a way that's pure animal. He holds me tighter, squeezing me, as if he's not sure I'm real.

I'm overcome to be with him again, to smell him again, to be held by him again. I clutch him back just as hard, pressing into his hands purely on instinct.

"Cragnorr, I'm so glad you're all right," I say, my voice cracking. "I missed you. I'm so sorry. I don't want anyone but you."

He nods in approval. He knows that it was a show, that Zake means nothing to me. Then he grabs the strip of fabric that's doing the bare minimum of covering my ass, and yanks them down my hips, tearing them. Suddenly, I'm bared to him from the waist down.

Something has changed in my ogre. Seeing that huge lump in his pants straining, his eyes focused on me—he's become nothing but pure, raging instinct.

"Mia," he growls low in his throat. He rips off the tie holding his pants on and that massive cock pops out, full and fat. Veins spider up the sides from the thick root, and it pulses as I stare. Liquid is dripping from that slit at the tip, and I think it's his bare hunger for me. The fury in his soul has taken over, the one hidden beneath the gentle giant, and it wants *me*. I'm throbbing between my legs, imagining where that immense thing of his will go.

Cragnorr grunts as he lifts me up by my bare ass, his strong hands digging into my flesh. I wrap my arms around his neck to hold on while he stumbles forward, until my back is up against one of the dirt walls. He breathes hard and fast as he holds me up with one huge arm, then reaches between my thighs with the other. His fingers find me surprisingly wet there, and without preamble, he slides them inside me.

Oh, how he feels. Those two fingers are so thick, so wide, that I struggle to accommodate him. But he doesn't relent, pumping them in and out of me, his palm dragging over my clit with every thrust. I moan as my head falls back against the wall, and his hand continues fucking me.

Then, he pushes in a third finger. My body fights back for a moment, too tight to allow it in, but he's determined. With shocking force, he wriggles all three fingers inside me, thrusting them in and out so fast that it's making obscene, wet sounds. My face falls into the crook of his neck, overwhelmed by how good he feels with how my pussy is desperately trying to stretch open for him.

Surely someone is going to hear us out there. But do I care if they do?

"Cragnorr," I whisper, my hips bucking against his invasion. I don't know what it is that I want, but I know I want more. I want him deeper. I want him completely, all of him, forever.

He groans against me as he spreads his fingers even wider, forcing me open. I cry out, desperate to obey.

And then, quite suddenly, he pulls his hand back. He holds up his fingers, my slickness reflecting in the thin band of light coming from above, and he shoves them in his mouth. His eyes fall closed as he sucks me off his hand. But when he opens them again, they're alight with a fire I've never seen, and his cock jumps against me. Whatever happened in that arena, it has driven him to something wild, something new and fearsome. Still, I know that he would never, ever hurt me.

He may be a monster, but he's *my* monster.

Cragnorr presses his cock between my thighs, groaning when the length of it slides along my sensitive center. Is he going to fuck me like this? My pussy tingles, and I gasp as he once more drags me over his shaft, lighting up every inch of my skin.

I need him. I need him as much as he clearly needs me right now. His eyes are bloodshot, and his chest is still bleeding from where the lion broke through his defenses, but none of that matters to him. Staring into my eyes, his lips curled in bloodlust, he lifts me up, and the thick, soft head of his cock rises until it's lined up with my slit.

"Cragnorr," I moan, hooking my thighs over his hips and pressing down, so he slips through my folds, to that wet place reserved for him. "Please."

With a victorious roar, Cragnorr slides me down over his cock. It happens all at once, this huge, soft object pushing its way inside me, stretching my edges wide and demanding I open for it. I cry out as it breaches me, and Cragnorr shoves himself as deep as he can, burying himself in my body like he was always meant to be there.

I sob his name as I stretch to accommodate him, and I'm so full that I'm spilling over. My ogre roars as he lifts me up, almost falling free of me, before he brings me down onto him once more. He sinks in, settling into the place where he belongs.

CHAPTER 14

CRAGNORR

The smell of her fills my nose as I fuck her. Her cries are music to my ears. The sight of her head fallen back, her mouth open, is a feast for my eyes. I don't care how much my chest hurts where the lion clawed me.

This is what I've always wanted, and I simply didn't know it.

How my cock pushes through her slick, powerfully tight cunt, I don't know, but I've never felt anything like it. I have to take her fast and hard, right now, before my body gives in to my pleasure and I finish too soon. She's so hot as she squeezes me, so soft as she wrings me dry, and a powerful surge is winding its way up my spine, something that will erupt.

My little human, who fits me perfectly, who keens with bliss every time I pound into her. This is what I was made for, I know now. I will put my cock in her every day for the rest of my life, and empty myself inside her instead of on the floor. Yes, that's what I want—all my sticky white spend buried deep in her, where my animal mind tells me it goes.

This sparks even more tinder inside me, and I bellow as I shove my cock even deeper inside her, now that she has opened for me.

"Cragnorr, Cragnorr," she moans, each of her cries escalating in pitch. My blood is singing with her voice, all my rage boiling up into claiming my woman, my Mia.

That's what she is. *Mine.*

When I abruptly unleash, shooting my seed deep into her, my body keeps going. No, I need her to gush around me like she did when I licked her. My cock wants to taste her sweet flavor, too. A river streams out of her as my hips keep pumping. Mia seizes my hair in her hands, tugging on it harder with every thrust. She's tightening up around me, squeezing me so hard, and I plow through it, using all of my strength and resilience though my cock is far, far too sensitive.

My beloved Mia, who will be mine until the end of time. I will fuck her again and again, my soul uniting with hers, her cries filling up my head with foggy bliss. I will tell her with all of myself how much I care for her, what she means to me, the way my life cannot possibly continue without her.

Then her whole body turns rigid, and she screams as I sink my cock deep. I can't help going off a second time when she clenches me like that, her mouth open in carnal pleasure. I fill her up again, thrusting once, twice more, as our fluids gush down her thighs.

When I can no longer move inside Mia's sweet, tight cunt, I sink to the ground on my knees with her in my arms, still lodged inside her. When I look down, I find she is red around where I've plundered her, that slit now spread wide to accommodate me and dripping with my spend.

My blood cools, and a peace I've never felt settles over me. Mia whines as I slowly work my cock free of her swollen cunt. I give her a concerned frown, but she just smiles and waves me off.

"Only a little sore," she says, kissing my cheek.

I bring her into my arms then and lie back on the floor, letting her use my body as a bed. Neither of us speaks as all my rage and lust finally abates.

I know now, deep in my soul, that I belong to her, and she belongs to me. That this is what was intended for us.

Now I just have to figure out how to get us both out of here.

Day turns to night beyond the trap door. I wonder how long they'll keep us here in the dirt, without food or water. I can make out a few stars through the crack in the ceiling when Mia finally wakes.

"Mmm," she murmurs, rubbing her cheek on my chest. I run a hand through her soft hair, letting it dribble between my fingers like water. "This is a shit hole, but at least I'm with you."

I curl my neck to kiss the top of her sweet head. Of course, I feel the same way. Already my body is responding to her lying on top of me, thinking of how perfectly she swallowed me up. My cock brushes her thigh, and Mia giggles.

"Is that it?" she asks. "Now that you've done it once, you're hooked?"

I nod, but it's even more than that. I thought my place in the world was as her guardian, but now I know it's at her side. It's slipping my cock inside her and holding her as she sleeps. These are things I feel in my bones, and I wonder if she feels it, too.

But what do they have planned for us? Why is the King keeping us here? Perhaps this is my reward for killing the lion. It's not the freedom I'm after, but I will accept this small gift.

My Mia is still without pants, which is an enticing offer. But I want to touch her—all of her. More careful now than I was earlier today, I slide the tiny wisp of fabric that covers her breasts up over her arms, which she eagerly tosses away. I roam her body with my hands, memorizing the teardrop shape of her tits, the dip of her belly button, the flare of her hips from her waist in the darkness.

She does the same to me, even playing with my nipples and making me gasp at this fresh sensation.

She's still covered in me, and the scent of us mingled makes me thick and hard. I seize her by the hips and she lets out a squeak of surprise as I drag her upward, so her knees are straddling my face. Here, I can inhale her even more deeply, and without preamble, I bury my mouth in her.

Mia moans as I attack her, thrashing that tiny bead with my tongue, then ducking down to drink up all the wetness dripping out of her. She makes even more sweet noises as I lick her faster, harder, until she's nearly at her peak. I slide my fingers between her legs, where they meet wet lips, her sweet cunt pulsing as I tease it. Then I push them inside her, and she lets out a cry. I continue my work until she's grinding her hips against me, begging, "Cragnorr, Cragnorr," over and over.

Fuck. I need to be inside her, before she meets her finish. I want her to seize around me while she cries out my name.

I pull her back down again so she's positioned over my groin. My cock nudges between the cheeks of her ass, letting her know what it wants.

She gives it to me. Rising up to her knees, Mia guides me from the crease of her soft rear to the dip between her thighs. When my cock settles at her tiny cave and gently presses in, she winces. I grab her waist to stop her, furrowing my brow in concern.

She shakes her head and pets my chest. "It's okay," she says. "I want you, Cragnorr. Now."

I can't deny her anything, so I obey, drawing her hips down gently. I watch in fascination as her cunt spreads for me, but she's still so, so tight that I have to move slowly. Mia tests each depth, her eyes rolling back in her head as I press in deeper, and deeper. When I'm only halfway inside her she rises up, teasing just the tip of my cock before swallowing me up again.

As she moves faster, those perfect breasts bounce. She takes me at her own speed, dominating me, owning me the way I did her. As her cries grow louder and her movements jerkier, I lift her hips with my hands, lending her my strength. I'm going to hold out this time, I promise myself, even as her moans and fluttering cunt threaten to set me off. I pluck her nipples and squeeze her ass, consuming every part of her.

It's when she screams my name, her thighs going taut, her body freezing over me so I have to start slamming her down on my cock, that I can't hold back any longer. I groan as I explode inside her, her beautiful cunt throbbing and milking me for all I have to give it.

Panting, Mia falls down on top of me, and buries her face in the hollow of my throat. We stay like that, my cock inside her, our breaths rising and falling as one.

I don't know when she'll be dragged away from me, but I'm going to enjoy every moment I have with her.

She examines my wound and shakes her head. "How do we get out of this?" she asks, voice barely above a whisper. Finally, my cock is soft enough that it slides out, and I'm surprised by how much liquid runs down my leg.

I shake my head, because I truly don't know. But I will find a way.

MIA

When the sun comes up again, we're both painfully hungry. We've been sitting side-by-side, Cragnorr's arm around my shoulders, waiting for what comes next. I'm afraid they'll make me leave him when they do finally come, and brace myself for it.

At last, a heavy lock turns, and the door opens. Six guards file in, and Cragnorr places himself in front of me.

"Woman," one of the guards says, shaking a hand at me. "You're leaving." Cragnorr lets out a warning growl when they come near. One of the guards reaches for his sword, the others tensing up to act.

I put a hand on Cragnorr's arm. "I have to go with them," I say quietly, "or they'll hurt you."

He responds by curling his hands into fists, preparing to fight.

"I'll be all right." I don't know if this is true, but I can't let my ogre get himself killed. "I've survived this long, haven't I?"

The tension doesn't leave Cragnorr's body, but he gazes down at me with a terrible sadness in his eyes. He pulls me into his arms, smelling my hair, clutching me as if we might never see each other again. I run a hand down his tusk, then kiss his nose before turning around and offering my wrists to the guards. They run a rope around them, and Cragnorr wails behind me as I'm led out the door.

"Disgusting," one of the guards says as I'm led away, mostly naked, clinging to my ripped clothes. We pass through a dark, dank room filled with metal cages, and inside them are people—two men and two trollkin, one green and one blue. I wonder if this is where they've been keeping Cragnorr.

What a horrid place to live, with no sunlight, chained and left in a cage.

Somehow I have to get him out of here.

Despite my blatant nudity, I pay close attention as the guards guide me up the stairs and out into the open. The door leading down into the holding area is wood, but locked with an iron bar. It would be challenging to get in there without a key.

Narria is waiting for me when we emerge, and the guards hand my rope over to her. She surveys me up and down.

"Not so innocent anymore," she says with a wry smile. Then she leads me away, to that isolated corner of the camp where I can bathe and, hopefully, find some fresh clothes.

When I'm in the tub, I clean myself between the legs and let out a whimper at the soreness there. Narria arches an eyebrow from where she sits nearby.

"How did you do that, anyway?" she asks, propping one elbow on the side of the tub. "That must be one monster of a cock."

My cheeks heat just thinking about it, how full I felt, how gloriously he wrung me dry.

She arches an eyebrow. "That good? Psh. And a virgin, too." She flings a towel at my head. "That's not fair."

I give her an odd look. "What isn't?"

"That you had a good time in the sack on your first try," she says irritably as I get out of the water and dry myself off. "Usually it's shit, you know."

She raids what appears to be the communal clothing exchange and returns with an even skimpier outfit than the last one. When I slip on the tiny, slinky bottoms, they ride up my ass.

"There's someone coming tonight," she says, gesturing at the silky harness she's handing me. It's barely enough to keep my nipples hidden. "He wants you to look good for our guest."

I shudder.

It's midday when I'm led to Zake's house with the leaning roof and misshapen walls. Narria knocks, and we hear a groan coming from inside. The door opens, and a bleary-eyed King answers wearing only a robe that's falling off his body.

He blinks when he sees me standing there, then his mouth curves up on one side. I don't like the sick, knowing look on his face.

"That ogre sure can make a woman scream," he says, revealing all of his stained teeth. "Now I see the appeal."

I say nothing.

Zake's smile widens. He beckons Narria and me inside, then flings off his robe and wanders his room naked for a few minutes, looking for what he wants to wear. Eventually, he chooses an embroidered jacket over his bare chest, and a pair of tight pants. He looks absolutely ridiculous.

"Come, come." He gestures at Narria, who stands at attention, having never even spared him a glance as he dresses. "Let's go greet them."

CHAPTER 15

CRAGNORR

Everyone stares at me as I'm led back to my cage and then tossed inside. This time I'm collared, much to my dissatisfaction, and no one treats my wound. But my blood is still hot with the feeling of Mia on top of me, around me, and I'm filled with a fresh, new strength. I may be in a cage again, but now, I have hope. I will get out of this horrid place so I can be with her again.

The moment the guards leave, the chattering among the prisoners begins.

"So you put your cock in the cunt?" the orc asks me with a knowing grin.

"We could hear her all the way in here," says Pa'zi, rubbing one of her tusks. "You did a good job for your first time."

It's none of their business. I sit down silently on the floor of my cage, leaning back and closing my eyes so I can imagine Mia on top of me again.

"How was it?" The orc shakes his bars as if to keep me awake. I glare at him. "Humans are so small. I've never even wondered what their cunts feel like."

Instantly I remember how her hot sheath squeezed me, how her pleasured keens filled me up to bursting. A small smile lifts my lips.

"That good?" The orc chuckles. "Not as good as a mate's cunt, though. Nothing is as good as that."

Pa'zi arches an eyebrow. "And you know this... how?"

I wonder what this word means, *mate*.

"Because I have one." The orc wraps his hands around the bars tightly. "She's out there, somewhere."

"So that's why you fight like it's your last day on earth." Pa'zi gives him a wistful look. "If you die, she dies."

All he does is nod, but I'm perplexed by this. Why would this *mate* of his die? Finally, I bring myself to ask, "Mate?"

The other two trollkin stare at me like I'm the biggest fool they've ever seen.

"You don't know?" Pa'zi asks, eyes wide. "Were you raised by wolves?"

I shake my head. Why would wolves have raised an ogre?

"Mates are life partners." The orc leans heavily on the bars. "They're your other half. Your everything. The purpose of your life." Here, his voice cracks, and his eyes fall to the floor. "Mine was going to be the mother of my whelps. She was carrying our first one when we were attacked. We had decided to move out of Kalishagg, away from the city, so we could raise it in my home-land." Though he's shielded himself carefully until now, I can see his armor break away as he remembers this lost dream. "Foolish. Out on the road, these fuckers found us, and you know the rest. She made it out, but they took me as a prize."

"At least you know she's still alive," Pa'zi says, and there's even a trace of pity in her eyes. "Or else you wouldn't be here."

I think about this. *Your everything. The purpose of your life.* That is my Mia, most certainly.

The orc stoops down in his cage to peer at my face. "Is that what you've found, ogre?" he asks with a pitying look. "Is that why you turned into a monster out there and killed that lion? You're protecting what's yours?"

I don't respond, because the truth of it terrifies me. If Mia is, in fact, this *mate*, then my death would mean hers, too.

"I hope for your sake that you haven't seeded her," the orc says, settling down on the floor. A deep pain fills his voice. "There is nothing so miserable as losing everything, all at once."

I give him a confused look. How could I have planted anything in Mia? She's a human woman, not garden soil.

Pa'zi laughs at me. "If he doesn't understand about cocks, cunts, *or* mates, what makes you think he understands how whelps are made?"

My heartbeat picks up speed. I was a whelp once, held in my mother's arms. But I don't understand what that has to do with cocks-in-cunts.

"Ahh." The orc offers me a sad smile. "You don't know, do you? When you pour all your seed inside an orcess or a trolless, sometimes, it takes root. Then it grows and grows inside her..." To illustrate, Pa'zi rubs her belly. "And becomes a whelp."

"Just like you were once," the trolless says with a wink.

My blood turns cold.

No. No, there's no possibility that I did this, that I planted a seed in Mia. But at the mere idea of it, of my spend finding purchase inside her and becoming a whelp made of both of us, my cock shivers.

I shake my head and press my thumbs to my temples. I would never have done it if I'd known. Would I?

I remember the fog of red, the driving need to kill that lion and save Mia. It had wanted only one thing to be sated, and it was her. I don't know that I could have stopped myself. That animal inside me… it wanted to shoot all of my seed as deep as I could, and I obeyed it. Now there's a chance that she has my whelp growing in her belly.

And I might never see her again.

My hands find their way under my collar, and I yank on it as hard as I can. I have to escape this place. I have to find Mia, who might be carrying our young, and get her out of here safely. A whelp deserves better than chains.

"Idiot," the orc grumbles. "There's no way you'll be able to escape. It's no use hurting yourself."

Fex is watching with keen interest as I tug and yank at my collar anyway. "What have you all been saying?" he asks in Freysian, tilting his head. "Something rather serious, it seems like."

I don't answer him. I try and try to free the collar, but it's too thick, too heavy. If I could just get it off, then I could easily bend the bars of my cage. I'll never be able to escape as long as this collar is holding me down.

"Not gonna work, buddy," Fex says, shaking his head.

He's right. It's no use. I'm trapped here, beneath the earth, longing for my mate—and hoping I haven't planted a whelp in her before I can get us out.

Mia

Zake's guests are not so marvelous as he made them seem. Outside the front gates of the town, a small caravan is waiting with a few bedraggled horses and half a dozen wagons, a few of them covered in fabric and tassels. A tall, skinny man emerges from one of the wagons, and his legs are impossibly long. He has to bend down to bow his head.

"Your Majesty," the man says dutifully. So, even outsiders humor the King.

"Have you brought me something exciting?" Zake says, much like a child would.

The man nods, and produces a gold trinket in the shape of an elephant. The King turns it over in his hands, mesmerized by its shine.

"This will do, I suppose," he says, and pocketing the elephant, gestures for the caravan to enter.

I am not introduced, but I am paraded past, and the new arrivals watch with keen interest. Goosebumps erupt across my skin.

After the guests have settled in and the sun has reached the horizon, the fires are lit and the beer is rolled out. Another party begins, though I'm not sure that the previous one ever actually ended.

I'm seated next to Zake at one of the long tables, with the skinny man on the other side. At first, both engage in merry festivities, until they start talking business. The outsiders have goods to trade, and the King is interested in their offer. I'm tuning it out until the visitor says, "And I've brought you a prize fighter for your... pit."

I perk up. Anything to do with a prize fighter could concern Cragnorr.

"A fighter?" The King thrums his fingers on the table thoughtfully. "Well, I have a new prize fighter, myself. Perhaps we should try them out."

The other man barks a laugh. "Well, as much as I would enjoy that, she might end up dead and then I'm out. You'll have to buy her first."

"Ahh." Zake nods. "I understand your game now, Masten. But

you'll have to do a better job of convincing me your fighter is worth it when I have a much more fearsome beast on offer."

"Beast?" the man called Masten asks, tilting his head like a stupid bird.

"An ogre, to be exact." Zake grins down at me knowingly. "I doubt your piddly human fighter can take him out."

The skinny man doesn't respond right away, but taps his chin, lost in thought.

"But how do you force a trollkin to fight?" asks Masten after a while. "You can't offer them their freedom."

A smile curls the King's lip. "Just need the right incentive." His eyes travel down to me, and that smirk grows wider. "I'm lucky in that I have something very special to my ogre." He grabs my rope and jerks on it, which nearly knocks me out of my chair.

Masten understands his meaning, and his eyes get wide. "An ogre and... a woman?" he asks. He takes a long drink of his beer, then leans in closer to Zake. I almost can't hear what he says next.

"Did you know that humans and trollkin can reproduce?" he whispers conspiratorially.

A stone falls in my belly. There's no way that can be. We're too different, right? The thought has never once occurred to me.

But Zake is instantly intrigued. "That's quite a story," he says, arching an eyebrow.

"It's true," Masten goes on. "When I was in Eyra Cove, it was more than just a rumor. Some of them lived there. It's an open secret."

I'm already bracing myself for what's coming when the King's eyes travel over to me. Fuck, fuck, fuck. There's no way Masten is telling the truth. He can't be.

Zake strokes his chin in mock-thoughtfulness. "So," he murmurs to me, leaning down close to my face so I can smell his awful breath. "Can that monster put a baby inside you?"

I clench my eyes closed, wondering if we've committed a

deeply foolish act. When Cragnorr filled me up, letting loose everything inside me, I was driven by pure instinct. Surely this strange man is wrong.

Narria, sitting next to me, frowns. "A half-ogre bastard?" she asks, disgusted.

"Exactly!" Zake gets to his feet, like he's about to perform for us. "Imagine. As big as that monster, but with a brain." He walks in a semi-circle around my chair, but I keep my eyes fixed on the floor, hoping against hope that he's wrong, that this can't possibly happen. "I'd raise it myself. Teach it to fight as soon as it could walk." He examines me all over as he completes his loop. There's a ringing in my ears as he talks, imagining myself carrying Cragnorr's baby, and then having it torn away from me. "A fighter who enters the pit willingly," Zake goes on, "who has the strength and the size to put on a good show, and the intelligence to be deadly."

Narria clenches my rope tighter. "You're not serious."

I can't even utter a sound.

"It's a brilliant idea," says Masten, clapping his hands together.

"All that to bring some excitement to the pit?" Narria asks.

"It's not *just* the pit," Zake says. "You know it and I know it. It's entertainment, it's a break from the monotony, and an excuse for the people to keep going. Who doesn't want to return from a long journey and watch some bloodshed?"

There's a click as Narria snaps her mouth closed, clearly understanding that Zake has made his decision.

I'm too stunned to speak. He plans to use me, like a brood mare, and Cragnorr, too. We are nothing but animals, nothing but *objects* to him.

When the evening's festivities are winding down, Zake takes my rope and bids the guests goodnight. He stops next to Narria as we leave.

"Tell Gru," he instructs. "Every three days, she will visit the ogre, and he should oversee them personally." The King studies me coldly. "If my dream can't happen, though... then I'll have no use for her anymore. Or him."

I can't cry now, in front of them—I can't give this horrible man the gratification. But deep inside, I'm dreading what's to come.

CHAPTER 16

CRAGNORR

Two whole days pass before the next arena fight. Once again I'm fed scraps, just enough to get by on.

When the battalion of guards comes to retrieve their victims, I'm not chosen. No, Pa'zi's and Bino's cages are the ones opened, and the human man eagerly steps out, thrilled for his chance to redeem himself. I don't understand how anyone could walk into that pit with such enthusiasm knowing it's kill-or-be-killed.

"Bye," Pa'zi says to us as she's led out. "If I don't see you again, it was my displeasure knowing you."

"Same to you," the orc says, and she laughs.

Pa'zi wields a morning star, the ball end covered in spikes. The moment the door falls open and they step out into the arena, the crowd goes wild.

"She's a favorite," Fex explains to me. "Fights like a demon."

I search the faces all around the edge of the pit for Mia, but she is not at the King's side like before.

I hope something terrible hasn't happened to her. I clench the bars of my cage tightly as I watch the fighters circle one another in the pit.

This has a poor ending, no matter what happens. I don't want to see either of them dead.

As he did in our fight, Bino lunges first. Pa'zi spins out of the way, the chain of her weapon spinning around her like a ribbon. It swings into Bino's back as he runs past her, and he lets out a horrifying cry. It happens so fast I can barely keep track.

Pa'zi springs away, as quick and lithe as a deer, as Bino stumbles forward. He quickly rights himself, but there's blood trailing down his spine.

"Bitch!" he snarls, and this time, he waits for her to come to him, instead. The trolless, already growing bored, rushes him with the ball of her morning star flying through the air.

Miraculously, Bino raises the flat of his axe just in time to protect himself. Pa'zi is momentarily unbalanced as her weapon fails to meet its target. In this small opening, Bino dives for her, striking with his axe.

She screams as it buries itself in her side. But even with a puncture wound deep in her flesh, she flicks her arm, sending her weapon sailing through the air. With all of his attention focused on doing damage, Bino doesn't even think to react defensively.

There's a terrible crunching as the spiked metal ball connects with his skull.

Bino stands there, the morning star lodged in his head, staring at nothing. Pa'zi whips her arm back and it disconnects, the spikes tearing free of his flesh. My heart wrenches as Bino's legs give way underneath him, and he collapses to the ground with only half of a face.

The crowd goes wild as Pa'zi attempts to stride proudly around the arena, but she's limping as her side bleeds. She makes her way back to the door where she entered, and there the guards lead her inside.

To my surprise, a healer is brought in to treat her.

"Can't let one of the King's fighters die," she mutters as the man stitches her up, then applies a poultice to the outside of the wound. She's given a pillow to lie on in her cage, and I wonder if she'll survive.

I watch as out in the pit, Bino's body is dragged away. He never made it long enough to get his freedom.

When will my time to go out into the arena come? Will they use Mia once again to taunt me? Will my body be dragged away someday, too?

I won't let that happen.

MIA

Over the next few days, Zake observes me keenly. He leaves me tied in the corner of his dingy little house, even when he leaves, and occasionally Narria comes to bring me food. At some point she convinces the King to let me stretch my legs.

"She'll be no good to you if she's weak and sick," Narria argues, and Zake rolls his eyes but agrees.

As Narria and I walk around the camp, I pepper her with questions. "Has there been another arena fight?" I ask, hoping to glean some information about Cragnorr's well-being.

Narria grunts. "Yes, but your ogre is not on the docket. He's too valuable now."

I know exactly what she means. The King wants him as a stud horse, and he can't risk him dying in the pit. My stomach is roiling in anticipation of this "visit" with Cragnorr. I long to see him, but the idea of what the King wants from us makes me nauseous.

I try to keep my nerves in check and take in what I can as we walk. The camp is perpetually busy, and even in the daytime people are drinking. There are arguments and laughter, and in one tent, just as loud, a man is moaning and crying out as he's pleasured. It makes a shudder run through me, thinking of what tomorrow holds.

But if these are the circumstances under which I can see him... My heart needs to be near Cragnorr again.

On our walk we pass the bolted door that leads down, into the dark chamber where the King is keeping him. There's someone posted outside, a woman sitting atop a barrel with a bored look on her face. I wonder if she has a key on her, or if she simply stands sentinel.

Once we reach the front gates, Narria turns around again and we continue back the way we came. There are two guards up in the tower, but one looks half-asleep. Perhaps I've overestimated them.

At the gates, a crew is loading up horses with supplies and yoking them to wagons. Narria stops to make chit-chat as they prepare for their journey. I gather that the bandits usually roam the mountain pass near here, waiting for travelers and caravans on their way to the lowlands. They take what they can in surprise attacks, and leave before their victims can even think to fight back. Sometimes they travel further afield to contested territory, where they can kidnap trollkin for the King's arena.

Once again we return to Zake's house, where I'm tied up in the corner.

It's hard to sleep that night. I'm tingling with anticipation at the idea of seeing Cragnorr again, and dreading what we'll have to do.

There's no way I can bring a child into this world just to be Zake's toy. The idea horrifies me down to my very bones. I need a plan.

CRAGNORR

I don't sleep well after watching Pa'zi murder Bino. Pa'zi's breaths come heavy in the cage beside mine, and I hope she makes it. And I can't stop wondering where Mia is—and why I didn't see her today at the arena.

After many hours of agonizing, I'm able to drift off, thinking of Mia sleeping on my chest. But not long after, I'm startled awake by the stout woman with the baton rapping on my cage.

"Come on, big guy," she says. "I have a special job for you."

I don't like the sound of this.

Clambering to my feet, the guards unchain my neck, then slap manacles on my wrists and ankles before leading me out. Instead of going toward the pit, as I expect, they lead me down, down to the same heavy steel door that kept Mia and I trapped in the chamber underneath the arena.

This time, when I go inside I find... a bed.

I blink at it, not sure what I'm seeing, and no one seems inclined to explain. A meal is brought for me, mostly meat. I'm surprised by this, too—but it also fills me with dread. What does that horrible man have planned now?

After I've finished eating, the tray is taken away. I wait, and wait, until suddenly, the door opens again.

In steps Mia. I rush towards her, ready to wrap her up in my arms again, but the miserable expression on her face stops me.

Something is very wrong.

Mia

I should be happy to see him. Overjoyed to be reunited with him, to get to touch him again. But it's poisoned.

By the time Cragnorr reaches me, the tears I've kept at bay have finally broken free. He stops in front of me, worry etched across his face. He brings his hand down to my cheek to wipe the moisture from my eyes.

I'm about to explain when Gru walks in the room behind me, and the door closes. There's suspicion in Cragnorr's eyes as the little man crosses to a chair that seems to have been supplied specifically for this purpose.

"Well?" he says, when we've both stood there staring at him for a few moments. "Go on."

Cragnorr's brow creases. I rub the tears off my face and turn to him, taking a deep breath before I say what I have to say.

"That bastard, the King," I whisper to him, and he leans down closer. "He wants... he wants to use us." Unconsciously my hand travels down to my belly, where I imagine that poor creature growing.

But Cragnorr won't understand. How could he? I've told him nothing about how babies are made. So, knowing Gru is listening, I try my best to express what the King wants. We're merely warm bodies, just tools. Cragnorr's confusion slowly fades into horror, and then anger as I tell him about the child that might be, and what Zake plans to use them for.

When I'm finished, Cragnorr bares his teeth at Gru, like he could rip the man's face off. The little idiot has the sense to look concerned.

"The King will just punish you if you try," I say, running my hand up and down my ogre's arm to cool him off. "Or me."

At this, Cragnorr's anger fades into misery. He sits down on the bed, dropping his head into his hands, and I fold my legs under me beside him.

"We don't have all day," Gru calls out. "Get started!" Cragnorr snarls at him. "Think of it this way," the nasty little man says, "as long as you're valuable, the King won't make you fight." Gru waves a finger tauntingly back and forth. "So do what you're told, dog, and you'll get to keep your hide and your woman. You should be grateful. Otherwise, you'd never see her again."

Cragnorr's eyes rise up to mine, heavy and sad, and I wish I could protect him from this. I put my hands on either side of his face, urging him to look at me.

"Just pretend he's not here," I say, stroking from his wild hair down his cheeks to his wide, stern jaw. "Pretend it's just me."

With a heavy breath, Cragnorr loops his arms around me and pulls me onto his lap. He buries his face in my hair, his tusks framing my head. His hands spread apart, one sliding up over my breasts, the other down to my hips. He breathes hard a few times, then his fingers halt and fist in my clothes.

There is no telltale lump rising up between my legs. No, my ogre is too anxious. He can kill a lion, but he can't force himself to do this.

"Gru," I snap. He's been staring at us, and I can't shake the feeling of his eyes on me. "Get out. Nothing will happen while you're here."

He gives me a firm shake of his head. "No way. The King told me to stay and watch. To make sure."

"Well, then the King isn't going to get anything out of him." I squeeze Cragnorr's big fingers with mine. "He can't be made to perform like a circus animal."

Gru glances between us irritably. Then, with a grunt, he gets up and walks to the heavy door. On his way out he looks at me over his shoulder.

"I'll be listening carefully, and I'll know if you lie to me. Don't mess this up, or the ogre will be the one to pay for it."

Then the door falls closed.

Neither of us speaks after he leaves. I gently run a hand through Cragnorr's hair, untangling it with my fingers. They haven't even let him bathe since he's been here.

"I'm sorry," I murmur to him, turning my head to whisper into his ear. "This isn't the way I want to be with you."

He just nods in understanding, and clutches me tighter. I wish instead we could be out in the forest again, just the two of us lying in the grass, exploring each other's bodies with an innocence we'll never get back.

"Mia."

The soft sound of his voice surprises me. He presses his lips to my shoulder as he curls down over me, his big hands covering my body. "Cragnorr? What is it?"

He doesn't answer for some time, kissing the hollow of my throat, working his way up to my earlobe.

"Mia, you..." He swallows hard. "You... are my *kagazen*."

I don't recognize this word.

"*Kagazen*?" I ask carefully.

"My one. My only. My everything." I think this is the most I've ever heard him speak at once. Cragnorr tucks his head against mine. "The one I was meant for, who was meant for me."

This must be a Trollkin word. I get the sense it means more than just spouse or partner. No, whatever it is, it's special to him.

When I think for a moment of finding Cragnorr in that tree, of lying with him in the grass, of how wildly he took me after the fight—I know he's all of that to me, too.

CHAPTER 17

MIA

I turn around in my ogre's lap until I'm straddling him, and I bring a hand up to his tusk so I can tilt his head down toward mine. Gently I brush my lips over his, and his eyes close as he lets me tease him. I nibble his lip until he opens for me, and then I sweep my tongue over the surface of it. His hands cup my back as he returns my kiss just as gingerly, sampling my mouth, exploring me with his tongue. My arms wrap around his neck to pull him in closer, trying to think only of Cragnorr, only the here and the now.

"We can't give him what he wants," I tell him in the quiet, keeping my voice low so Gru can't overhear us.

Cragnorr shakes his head. He, too, refuses to create a child sentenced to what Zake has planned. But Gru will know if we don't do what we're here to do.

"Pull out at the end," I tell him. "Right when you think you're going to shoot off..."

His eyes search mine, and then he nods in understanding.

"Then we can't make a baby," I tell him, rubbing his hand. "But... maybe we still can someday. When we're free."

Cragnorr takes my cheeks in his hands and slowly, lowers his head to kiss me. I'm surprised when he picks me up, then settles me down on my back, my head on the pillow. He towers above me, only the hanging lamp lighting his rough features and big, sturdy body. He brings his finger to my lips, tracing the lines of them. Then he trails down my chin, to my throat and collar bone. He kisses there, right where his finger is pressed, and peppers more kisses down my front. When he reaches my belly, he stops there, sighing to himself.

Were things different, I think, I would very much like to see what kind of child we could make together.

His hand ducks under my tunic and then explores upward again, pausing to cup my breast. Abruptly he pulls the tunic up, and I slide it over my arms, revealing me to him. Cragnorr simply looks at me, studying me, and it's as if I can feel him touching the edges of my soul. He crouches down over me, shadowing everything, and kisses the valley between my breasts. With infinite patience he ventures out to my nipple, bringing it between his lips and grazing over the tip with his tongue.

My hips spasm under him as bursts of heat radiate out from where he's touching me, all of it streaming down and gathering between my legs. Cragnorr continues his slow exploration, like he's making up for the tenderness we didn't have the first time. He slides down my trousers, slow and methodically, until I'm fully naked in front of him.

But he's only interested in one thing: the place at the juncture of my thighs. Hunger has turned his features severe as he gently pushes them apart. He leans down, and brushes over my outer layers with the tip of his tongue. I shudder at just the promise.

Cragnorr isn't gentle any longer when he takes me with his mouth. It's like he's an animal starved, the way he licks and sucks me, soon dropping his hand down to press his fingers inside me. As he pumps his hand and devours me with his mouth, I'm clinging to him, until the avalanche comes and sweeps me down the mountainside. He groans as he licks his wet fingers, and I shiver underneath him.

When I've finally gained my sense of reason back, I sit up in front of Cragnorr and push on his chest. He doesn't budge, giving me a curious look.

"Lie down," I tell him, pushing again. He obeys, trusting in me, but still wondering what I have planned for him. I carefully untie his pants, then scoot them down his hips until...

There it is. His huge, dark green cock slides out, thick and bulging. It twitches when I take it in one hand, my fingers barely reaching halfway around. When I begin to stroke it with both hands, Cragnorr's head falls back and he groans.

But that's only part of what I have planned for him. While he's not looking, I bring my mouth down to the soft, thick head, and tentatively run my tongue over the tip.

His eyes fly open and his head shoots up as I taste him again, licking up the salty, sweet seed dribbling from his slit. He doesn't try to stop me as I lean over and open my mouth wider, taking him inside it.

The noise Cragnorr makes when I swallow him is almost inhuman. He looks panicked, like he doesn't understand the sensation of my lips on him. I push him back down to the bed as I withdraw my mouth, swirling my tongue around that head before taking in more again. His hips snap under me, and he brushes my hair with his hand. Stroking the base of his cock at the same time that I'm bringing him into my throat earns me a deep moan.

I want to show him all the pleasure imaginable while I can. I want him to enjoy our time together, even if it was forced upon us.

It isn't long before he's twitching and jerking under me, and his cock swells up so huge inside my mouth that my jaw strains and I have to cough it out. White fluid shoots out across my face and lips, painting me, marking me.

He's mine as much as I am his.

Cragnorr's eyes are wide when he props himself up on his elbows to look down at me. I crawl up the bed until I'm lying along his side, and he rolls over to gather me up in his arms. He buries his face in my hair, squeezing me tight in a way that tells me he's grateful.

A knock suddenly comes at the door. "Get going!" Gru shouts from the other side. I wince and curl up tighter against Cragnorr, wishing all of this was different.

CRAGNORR

The way she took me into her mouth, I forgot for a moment why we're here. The only sensation I could feel was *her*, my Mia, my mate.

Still, my cock longs for her warm cunt. I had hoped I could delay, that I could enjoy her longer before they took her away, but now... we don't have time. That awful man will return, and if we haven't performed our task, who knows what they'll do to her?

While my mind tries to have patience, my cock is already stiffening up again and nudging at her belly. This time I'll take her gently and show her what she means to me.

I kiss her softly, pouring everything I feel into it, and her mouth readily parts for me. I drag my hand down her side, over the curve of her hip and the swell of her butt, around her strong thighs to the soft wet place between her legs that sings my name. She's still moist and tender from my attentions earlier, so all I need to do is tantalize that small button between her folds to make her mewl with need.

Gripping her tight, I roll us over so I'm wedged between her spread thighs. My cock knows exactly where it's intended to be.

I watch in awe as I guide it toward the cavern that was designed for me, and the head vanishes into her. The lips of her cunt spread as I push deeper in, and she answers with a moan.

"Cragnorr," she gasps, grabbing her own breasts and squeezing her nipples. "Please, more."

I can't deny her anything, so I obey, thrusting further inside her. Her incredible body welcomes me, giving way easily. Her small cunt can't take all of me, so I pause when I meet resistance and draw back. My cock emerges slick with her, shining under the dull lamplight. When I plunge in again, her eyes flutter closed and a stream of pleasure spills from her lips. I repeat this slow motion, over and over, searching for what she likes most. Her legs clench tight around my hips, drawing me even deeper inside her, and I drop forward onto my elbows as the pure sensation of her overwhelms me.

A thought occurs to me: that tiny button hidden between her folds is the most tender part of her body. I wonder what would happen if I touched it while I was inside her?

Sitting back, I continue the steady pumping of my hips, drinking in the sight of my cock opening her up, exposing everything to me. Her little body can't even take my whole length.

I brush the pad of my finger over that small pearl of pleasure, and Mia's eyes fly open, her hips abruptly jerking against mine. "Oh, Cragnorr," she whimpers, grabbing onto me frantically, her fingers curling like claws in my flesh. "Oh, just like that."

I'm delighted by her reaction, so I rub her quicker, increasing the pace of my thrusts to match. Her cunt tightens around me, and I have to breathe through my nose to keep from reaching my finish too soon. She feels like nothing else on this earth, like the most perfect bliss, and I think I could drown in her forever.

The faster I move, the louder her cries grow, until suddenly she falls silent. Her eyes find mine and they're huge and round, and she clenches me so tight my cock can barely move. A shiver of bliss winds its way from my throat down to my balls as I tip over the edge—and only at the last moment do I remember why we're here, and what Mia told me to do.

They want me to sow my seed inside her, to give her a whelp I'll never get to meet. The fury washes over me so powerfully that I pull out as fast as I can, and my spend arcs through the air to land on Mia's breasts. I groan as even more seeps out, dripping onto her belly.

Mia blinks a few times, looking down at where I've splattered her, and her face falls. She is remembering, too, how we are being listened to, how our captors only see us as animals to be bred. Her eyes are shining, so I embrace her with all the strength in my body. She shivers against me as she struggles not to cry.

The metal door creaks when it opens. I quickly wipe her off with one of the blankets, so our overseer won't notice I spent my seed on top of her instead of inside her. The lanky man lets out a disgusted sound as I remain crouched over my woman, knowing they'll take her away from me, but relishing every last second I spend with her warm body against mine.

"Get up, brute," he growls as a squad of guards arrange themselves behind him. Raising my hands in the air, I climb off of Mia, even as she reaches for me to return.

Once I'm dressed, they clamp the manacles on me, then snap the collar around my throat and drag me out of the room. All I hear as I leave is Mia's sobs, and my heart breaks as she fades away behind me.

My Mia. We must escape this place. I need my mate by my side, free from this horror—and I will do anything to get it.

CHAPTER 18

MIA

I break apart when Cragnorr is forced to leave me. All I want is to curl up at his side, circled by his tree-trunk arms, and fall asleep that way. I want to hear his breath next to me, and wake up to his cheek against my hair.

But now I'm alone, and Gru is dragging me to my feet and forcing me to dress before tying the rope around my wrists. He snaps at me to stop crying, but I can't keep it inside this time.

At least I know I'll see Cragnorr again in a few days, but that does nothing to quell the feeling that something very important has gone missing.

I remember when he emptied himself on my belly, and wonder how long the King will wait when I never get pregnant. Will he realize we're fleecing him? If he does... what will he do to Cragnorr? Or *me*?

Before, I thought about plans. I watched guard rotations and plotted routes around the camp where I might not be seen, should I manage to get away from Zake's house in the middle of the night.

But now, as I'm led back there and tied up in the corner, I simply feel empty and bottomless. The world could swallow me up, and no one would notice.

The days pass horribly slow, plodding along one agonizing minute at a time. When I next see Cragnorr, Gru doesn't try to stay and watch. He gives us a strange look as he leaves, almost like he pities us, then bolts the door closed behind him.

Cragnorr lies on the bed next to me, holding me and kissing my forehead, until our babysitter raps on the door and hollers at us to get a move on.

Again I ask him to lie on his back, and again I wrap my lips around his soft cock until he's hard and throbbing in my hands. This time I crawl on top of him to sink down on it, bringing it inside me and relishing the feeling of being whole again. Cragnorr moans and gasps underneath me, clutching my hips and ass in his hands as I take him slow. When my thighs wear out, Cragnorr gets onto his knees and guides me into the same position, so he can slide in from behind. Once again he flicks the pad of his finger over my clit while he fucks me, claiming me.

And once again, after he's ejaculated everything onto my back, they come and take him away.

I wish I could sleep beside him, or even eat a meal with him. Instead, Zake watches me as I try to get comfortable on the floor despite the bindings on my wrists. They're always red now from me moving around in the night.

"Let me sleep in Narria's tent," I ask him once, because anything would be better than this. At least with Narria, she'll speak to me, make conversation with me.

But no, the King wants to watch me break. He simply smiles at me.

"I can't keep an eye on you there," he says with a yawn, helping himself to some fresh fruit while I watch from the corner. He tosses me half of an apple, and it skitters across the floor, not even close enough that I could grab it. "I will be the first to know when your blood doesn't arrive, and then this little game will be over."

It's difficult not to let the hopelessness inside me, but late at night in the darkness, I can no longer keep it at bay. I cry, thinking of Cragnorr's arms, of sleeping in the grass, of the bright sky overhead. How long has it been since he saw sunlight?

My ogre. My lover. My best friend.

CRAGNORR

"How are your little *visits?*" the orc asks. His name, I've eventually learned, is Vagenn. He acts like this is a closely-guarded secret, perhaps fearing it might lead someone back to his mate. I understand his protectiveness over her now. The misery I feel when I'm apart from Mia is endless, a void that continues on forever in front of me.

I don't have an answer for him. Seeing Mia is like seeing the sun again, like stepping out into the real world. When she's gone, the weight of her absence is crushing, and I stagger under it. Locked in this cage down underground, we have no grasp of the days, and so it seems random when the short woman with the metal rod comes to get me.

"At least you can see your mate," Vagenn grunts after a time. "I'll never see mine again."

"I'll probably have to kill you first," pipes up Pa'zi, who has at least survived the worst of her injury. Her poultice hasn't been changed in some time, though, and I worry for her.

Vagenn simply shrugs. "I've come to terms with that," he says, though his eyes are sad. "But I will hold out as long as I can."

It's not that he fears his own death, but that of his mate. When I am no longer useful to the King, will he sentence me to the same fate? When I die, will I take Mia with me?

One day, a new victim is brought in and tossed into Bino's old cage. She's human, not particularly tall, but with shoulders as wide as the orc's. She says nothing to us as she's locked in and left to rot, and there is no welcome from Fex.

After a few hours have passed, she suddenly turns around in her cage and grabs the bars. "I'm not staying here," she growls. She has short, dirty yellow hair and her eyes are as hard as rocks. "You're content with this?"

"There's no choice about it," says Fex.

She laughs scornfully. "Weakling."

"What about this guy?" Fex asks, gesturing at me. "He could break out, but he gets to fuck twice a week, so he's happy to stay."

I glare at him. There is no way out of here, not as long as I stay collared.

The new woman's eyes drift over to me. "That thing?"

"He can understand you." Fex settles back into his cage. "So watch your mouth."

This draws the woman's curiosity. "Say something," she insists. "If you can speak Freysian."

I roll my eyes, a gesture I learned from Bino, and lean back against the bars to close my eyes. I sleep as often as possible when I'm not with Mia to make the time pass faster.

"Hmm," the woman says. "Curious."

Fex shrugs. "He's not very talkative. Not unless his lady is about to get eaten by a lion."

I cast him a deadly look, hoping he'll get the message and keep his mouth shut.

"His lady?" The woman arches an eyebrow at me. "As in, a human?"

Fex bares all of his teeth when he smiles, but like I asked, he doesn't answer. Not that she hasn't already answered her own question.

The newcomer looks at me with fresh eyes as I try once again to fall asleep. But I've barely dozed when our jailor appears, rapping her baton on our cages.

"You," she says, pointing at the newbie. "It's your turn. The King paid good money for you, and wants to see what you can do." Then she turns to Vagenn. "And you..." Maybe the orc can't understand her, but he knows what's coming anyway. He closes his eyes and leans his forehead against the bars. "This will be perfect. A human maiden up against a monstrous trollkin?" The woman with the baton wiggles her fingers. "Tantalizing!"

The guards approach and cuff Vagenn, then drag him out of his cage. As they lead him away, he glances over his shoulder at me. "Get out of here, ogre," he says. "Get your mate the fuck out of here, whatever it takes."

"Don't give up already," Pa'zi calls to him. "We know nothing about this bitch. You can take her."

Vagenn simply shakes his head. "I just hope fate lets my mate live. And then, maybe someday in the world beyond this one, I can see her and my whelp again."

I grip the bars as he steps out into the harsh sunlight of the pit to the sound of hollers and cheers. He doesn't plan to come back.

The new woman is led out next, and the guards toss them weapons. Vagenn wields an axe, while the newbie is handed nothing but a small dagger. How could she possibly defend herself with that? Perhaps she's the one who's been sentenced to her death.

When Vagenn is free of his shackles and so is she, they circle one another, each daring the other to go first. They're both light on their feet, which surprises me for an orc as big as Vagenn.

Then, like a flash of lightning, the woman crosses the pit and leaps on him like a cat. It's instant, before he can even think of defending himself. The force of it knocks Vagenn to the ground with a loud *oof.*

Now crouched over him, she raises the small knife in her hand up above her head. Before the crowd can even scream, she buries the dagger in Vagenn's chest.

Mia

It's been nearly three weeks since we arrived in this awful place, and I should have bled by now—but still no sign of my visitor.

I try not to think too hard about it, in case Zake reads it off my face. But the idea that we've already failed, that Cragnorr and I conceived before this game even started, haunts me into my dreams.

I've wondered if I could fake it by cutting into my thigh, but the daggers he keeps on his pile of jewels are too far away.

"It's like lions and tigers," the King says one night, lounging on his pillows and drinking wine. "The liger is quite a magnificent creature. Bigger than either of them. No one knew you could breed them together until my daddy did." He likes to mention his father, frequently, even though the man is long dead. "It's too bad your ogre killed it. Maybe I'll try to capture a bear next."

As soon as Zake knows the truth, Cragnorr's life could be forfeit. Unless he wants to keep us, and continue making more—

I can't think like that. I have to hold onto hope, or I'll slip away into darkness.

One day, the King returns late, and seems deeply disappointed.

"What a miserable fight," he grumbles. "No showmanship at all. And she came with a pedigree." Then a smile turns up his lip. "I thought she'd make it last longer."

Disgusting. I've had to listen to him jack off a few times, which is its own kind of torture. But at least he doesn't use me to sate his needs.

"You should look happier," Zake says, tugging me to my feet by the rope. "You get to see your ogre today."

I can't help the rush of pleasure I feel at the idea. Whenever we're apart, it's like I'm being pulled towards him, right through the ground.

"You like that, don't you? That fat ogre cock?" Zake laughs. "All right, I'll hand you off. Gru!"

Gru and I have almost reached a truce. He knows I won't put up a fight if he treats me with some dignity.

"The two of you aren't getting up to any funny business, are you?" Gru asks as he leads me down underground, past the room full of cages. I see that one of the two trollkin is now gone.

I wonder if that was the fight that upset Zake so much.

"Funny business?" I ask.

"You know what I mean." Gru shakes his head. "If you and the ogre are trying to pull the wool over His Majesty's eyes, it won't work. He *will* punish you."

So he knows that Cragnorr and I have not been obeying orders. I try to repress the shiver that travels through me.

"Thanks," I say in answer as I'm led in through the heavy metal door. It's all too late anyway.

Cragnorr waits for me on the other side, and my relief at seeing him after the last few days alone, stewing in my miserable thoughts, overwhelms me. Gru unties my wrists, then leaves the way he came.

The moment he's gone, I crumple to the ground. Concerned, Cragnorr kneels down next to me. His yellow eyes search mine, trying to find what's wrong. I fall into him and he catches me, pulling me in close.

I don't know how to tell him, but I have to. He should be the first to know. Once the King finds out, we may never be able to see each other again.

"Cragnorr," I begin, my voice trembling. "We already did it. There's nothing we can do to stop it now."

He tilts his head down to look at me, confusion in his eyes.

"Remember down here? After your fight?" Saying it out loud suddenly makes it real. I'm pregnant, and I'm trapped here. I can't help the sobs that take over me. "It happened," I say through my tears. Cragnorr is very still. "I didn't know it was even possible. I didn't think it could, not when we're so different. But my period hasn't come yet, and I think that means that—" A quiet sob tumbles out of me. "I'm already pregnant, Cragnorr."

"Mia." His low, quiet voice startles me. My ogre pulls away so he can look me in the eyes, and his are red around the edges. "You will have a whelp? *My* whelp?"

I nod slowly, tears spilling down my face.

A sad smile breaks across Cragnorr's face. He kisses me, and trails his hand down my body to my belly.

"Here," I say, resting my small hand over his much bigger one. For this one moment in time, I pretend that this is a celebration, that we've done something amazing and it belongs to us. But it only lasts for a moment before I can't hold in the regret any longer.

When I finally break down, Cragnorr hugs me, squeezing me as tight as he can, and I burrow deep into his chest. This might be the last time I get to touch him at all.

CHAPTER 19

MIA

I'm quiet as Cragnorr undresses me, and then peels off the filthy pants he's been wearing since we were both taken captive. He looks embarrassed, running a hand through his dirty hair. It is a foul kind of cruelty, not to even allow him the dignity of bathing.

As he sits on the bed, his eyes downcast, I crawl into his lap. His arms slip around me, encompassing me, as he buries his face in my neck. I hold him like that as he shakes, as we both mourn something that should have been beautiful.

When Cragnorr's tears ebb, I urge him to look up at me, and then kiss him thoroughly. He groans as I nibble his lower lip, and I sense him growing hard underneath me. I drag myself back and forth across his lap, so his cock slides through that wet place between my thighs. He moans, his arms wrapping tighter around me, telling me all the words he feels but cannot say. Though we take our time teasing each other, grinding my clit against his length, Gru doesn't knock at the door.

"At least now," I say, leaning closer to his ear, "you don't have to pull out."

Cragnorr nods in understanding. His hands grow bolder, cupping my ass, glancing over my nipples with his thumbs and then plucking them, one at a time.

"That's how I'll feed our baby," I tell him, wrapping his whole hand around my breast.

His eyes are wide in wonder as he investigates them further, licking them and twirling the nipple around in his mouth. I tangle my hands in his hair and moan, pressing my hips even harder against him. When I can't take any more, I reach down between us and lift myself up onto my knees, then fit him between my wet, swollen folds.

Cragnorr lets out a moan as I bring him inside me, as far as I can on the first thrust. Again I rise, and again I lower myself onto him, swallowing him up, bringing him home to me. I imagine that we're no longer in this dark room, on this tiny, dirty cot, but instead have just bathed in a lake and now lie beside it, both of us basking in our joy and excitement at what we've created together.

I wrap my arms tight around his neck, holding him as close to me as I can, squeezing my eyes closed to envision a different reality. He gasps every time I spear myself on his cock, his huge hands eclipsing my body as he squeezes and strokes me.

But soon the animal takes over him, and he uses those big hands to push me down onto my back, before pulling my thighs apart and gripping my legs while he takes me. We're so soaked with our need, with our boiling desire for each other, that each pump of his powerful hips makes an obscene sound. I'm crying out, tangling my hands in his hair, gripping his shoulders tight as he seeks out the place inside me that will make me forget everything else.

Then, suddenly, he's swelling up even fatter, even thicker inside me, and his big, amber eyes go wide. I'm so full with his cock that it drags me over the edge, hurling me into nothingness. Cragnorr bellows as he finishes, jamming himself deep and spilling himself inside me as I sob out his name.

While we lie there panting, our sweat mingling, he trails a hand over my belly as if drawing something.

"Even if they never know you," I say quietly, "I'll make sure to tell them everything about you. How wonderful and perfect you are. How strong, in every way."

Cragnorr's eyes are shining with moisture as he lifts his gaze to mine, protectively spreading his hand across my stomach. His shoulders tremble, and I realize that I'm crying, too. He hugs me tight, rubbing his forehead against mine, leaving kisses across my nose and cheeks and licking away my tears.

Gru comes in only minutes later, the guards following. Cragnorr gets up, protecting me with his body. He grits his teeth and curls his hands into fists.

"Don't," I beg him. "There are too many of them."

But my ogre is fierce, and his new knowledge has turned him into an animal. He will protect what's his. When they try to shackle him, he swings one of his huge arms, knocking a guard to the side.

"Cragnorr, stop!" I try to tell him, but he claws at his captors. They snap on his manacles, and with a hard jerk, they knock him to the floor with a horrible *thud*. I sob his name as they drag him out of the room. "I'm sorry," I call after him. "I'm sorry."

"My Mia." He shakes his head, and furious determination crosses his face as he's dragged away. "My *kagazen*."

Then the heavy door falls closed behind him.

Cragnorr

My mate is carrying my whelp. And I'm leaving her, perhaps forever, if the King finds out that it's now growing inside her.

I may never see her, or them, while I'm alive.

Rage fills me as I leave Mia behind. I can't stand by and let them tear us apart. I fight as hard as I can all the way back to the holding room, gnashing my teeth and yanking on my chains. Other guards are called in to help restrain me and shove me into my cage. Then they slam the door behind me and stalk out, muttering curses about *the ogre*.

I shake the metal bars, my vision red at the edges as I think about Mia, all alone, holding our whelp in her arms. How dare they keep me from her? The fury spreads, filling my veins like fire. I would kill them all should I get my hands on them.

The thought of Mia consumes me as I look for a way out. I can't be trapped here any longer. I have to find my mate and escape before I become Vagenn.

At least this time they couldn't get a chain onto my collar.

"Easy, buddy," Pa'zi says next to me, holding up her hands. "You're going to hurt yourself like that."

I roar at her, as if words are now beyond my reach. All I have left is my wrath.

"What's with him?" the new woman asks, watching curiously.

Fex narrows his eyes at me. "What did they do to her, ogre?"

"Mine!" I bellow, wrapping my hands around the bars and pulling on them as hard as I can. "Mia is *mine!*"

It's not until Pa'zi gasps that I realize I've bent the metal bars of my cage. I stare down at them, now curved where I put all of my force into my hands.

A fresh wave of need washes over me—the need to get out of here, to find my mate, to save my whelp. I grab the bars of the cage door in my hands and pull as hard as I can, bracing all of my weight against them.

Mia. My purpose. I will fight my way out of here until I die.

I howl one more time, all of that hot rage pouring into my muscles. The bars of the cage creak as I funnel it into this one thing.

"Holy fuck," Fex says, backing up a few steps. "Remind me to never get you angry."

Underneath my massive hands, the door finally gives. The latch snaps off as the bars bend beyond recognition. I shove it open, hurling it out of the way, and it skates across the stone floor with a terrible screech.

I can only think of one thing: getting to Mia.

"Wait, big guy!" Pa'zi calls out. "Do you have a plan? You're not going to make it out of here alive."

I barely hear her. None of them matter. I have one goal and one desire, and I will destroy anything in my way.

"Hey." A quiet, feminine voice breaks through the fog. "Over here."

I glance up to find the blonde woman standing at the door of her cage. Her voice sounds so much like Mia's that I pause to listen to her.

"Let me out," she says. "I can help you find her."

"Bullshit!" calls Fex. "You don't know where she's being kept."

"Yeah, but maybe together, we have a better shot." She keeps her eyes on me. "Come on. You want your woman back, right?"

I pant heavily, trying to think through the words she's saying. She could help me find Mia?

"I know more than she does about the camp," Fex calls out. "If you let anyone go, it should be me."

The conscious part of my head says, *listen to them.* I am alone, it's true, and those guards from earlier will take me down if I'm faced with all of them on my own. But maybe against the four of us...

"What's going on?" calls out Pa'zi in Trollkin. She can't understand anything the humans are saying. I go to her cage first, heat still pulsing in my veins, and grab onto the door. I plant my hands between two bars and squeeze them apart as hard as I can.

The metal gives, and the lock snaps off.

"Whoa," Pa'zi says, looking down at the mangled metal. She steps through, then stares up at me, cocking her head. "What are you?"

Without a word I do the same to Fex's cage, and then at last, the newbie's.

"I'm Marta," the blonde woman says. She gestures down the hall toward the stairs. "If we go out that way, we're dropped right into the middle of camp." That might not be wise, but my blood is still pumping hot, and I need to find Mia.

"We should go through the pit," Marta says.

"*Through* the pit?" Fex glances back at his cage. "Fuck. You shouldn't have let me out. Now I'm gonna get caught and beaten with all of you idiots."

"There's another door in the pit," Marta explains, ignoring him. "Where they took that orc's body away." She tilts her head at me. "Can you break down the big door into the arena?"

I don't need to be asked twice. I turn around and barrel into it with my shoulder. It's meant to be opened from the outside, so the middle gives easily.

I smash through it, splintering the wooden door in half, and find myself in the pit. The others follow through behind me.

"Better than a cannon," Fex says with a whistle.

Marta runs ahead of us and points out the door on the opposite side. "That's the one," she says. "It must lead somewhere they can dispose of the bodies."

"So, a catacomb, is what you're saying," Fex deadpans. "I'm going to vote no on the catacomb."

Ignoring him, I stalk across the arena, toward the big door. It's our best shot. Maybe it leads out of the camp altogether, wherever they dispose of the bodies.

Readying myself, I charge into the door, slamming it with all of my weight. It cracks right down the center, splitting in half like a log under an axe. We're making a lot of noise, so we have to hurry before someone comes to investigate.

Marta slips into the tunnel first, which is pitch black inside. I follow her, with Fex and Pa'zi close behind.

"Where are we going, ogre?" asks Pa'zi, giving the two humans a doubtful look as we descend into the darkness.

I shake my head. She can come or she can stay—it's of no concern to me. I only have one goal, and it's to find the way out, and bring Mia with me.

As we walk deeper into the tunnel, Pa'zi grunts and finally follows along. I can't see anything, but I push onward, because this is the only chance we have. I feel along the walls, and we bump into each other from time to time as we make our way carefully.

There's a loud clatter. "Fuck," Fex hisses. "What was that?"

"Probably bones," Marta says in a bored tone. "Keep going."

I'm also kicking small objects as we make our way, and I try not to think about what they are. I try not to imagine Vagenn's body here, or Bino's, but the stench tells me they likely are.

"Awful," says Pa'zi, squeezing her nostrils shut. "Humans are animals."

Finally, up ahead, I spot a tiny band of light. I break into a jog, pushing ahead of the others as we get nearer.

It's a grate in the ceiling, moonlight shining through, but blocked off with bars.

"Damn it!" Fex stomps one foot. "We're so close, and then this?"

I shake my head. I'm not letting one piece of metal stop me now. I gesture at Pa'zi to come closer, and she peers up through the grate.

"Need help, ogre?" she asks. I nod, and she crouches down, offering her hands as a step even though she's still injured. Marta and Fex seem to gather what she's doing, and Fex imitates her. Once I'm lifted a few feet off the floor—and Fex groans miserably under my weight—I seize the bars of the grate and yank as hard as I can.

The metal bends, just enough that the edges are pulled away from the dirt. I yank again, and stumble backwards as the grate comes crashing down on top of me. Fex and Pa'zi are both knocked to the ground as I go sprawling, and the metal grate bounces off my belly. I gasp as the wind is knocked out of me.

Marta lets out a little cheer. "You did it!" When I manage to sit up again, she slaps me hard on the back. "Now we just have to figure out how to get up there."

Without asking, I pick her up around the waist and heave her into the air, high up above my head. She lets out a cry of surprise.

"Grab on, idiot!" calls up Fex. Marta obeys, hooking her arms over the porthole above us, and pulling herself up. Once she's there, she takes a quick look around.

"We're not far from the wall," she calls down to us. "Hurry up, before they see us."

"Then help me out!" snaps Fex. Marta gets down on her belly and holds her hands out, so Fex can go next.

Pa'zi watches this all with wide eyes. "What about you?" she says to me. "How are you getting out?"

I shake my head. I'm not going.

"What?" she asks in disbelief. "You're helping us escape, but you're not coming?"

"Mia," is all I say. Then I pick up Pa'zi, too, even though she's quite a bit bigger and heavier, and heft her over my head. She grabs onto the ledge, then hauls herself up without any help from the others.

"You next," says Marta, holding a hand out to me. "Maybe if all three of us pull him together?"

"Fine," says Fex, also crouching down to offer me his hand. "We can sure try, but he's a big boy."

I shoo them off. Now that we have a way out, I have to go back and get Mia.

I will never leave her behind, never again.

"Ogre!" Marta snaps at me. "This is your chance. Freedom. Don't throw it away for some girl."

She's wrong. It will never be freedom for me without my mate, without my whelp, without my everything.

Pa'zi grabs Marta's arm and shakes her head, even though they can't understand each other.

"We're leaving him," Fex says sharply. More lights are appearing overhead. "We have to go. Now." He glances down at me one last time, and gives me a pitying look. "I hope you make it out of here, you big oaf."

Then Marta and Fex are gone, leaving only Pa'zi. She gives me a small wave.

"Take care of yourself and your mate," she says, giving me a quick salute before she vanishes, too.

I turn around and head back the way I came at a quick lope. I don't have much time. But I know I'll find Mia. I have to.

The moment I step back out into the pit... that's when I hear someone shout.

"They got out!" It's two of the guards I've become so familiar with. But if there's only a pair of them, perhaps I still stand a chance.

One raises his gun and points it at me, but he's too far away to get a sure shot. So I run. I race towards them across the dirt floor of the pit, and the gun fires. It barely misses, howling past my ear.

Then I'm on top of him, smashing him into the ground. While he's stunned, I reach out for the second guard and yank her down by the leg. I grab her as I get to my feet, and hurl her over my head into one of the cages inside.

She falls to the ground, unmoving.

"Fuck!" the first guard groans in pain. He starts shouting. "Ogre! The ogre got out!"

I have to keep him quiet. I land a foot right to his head, shattering his jaw.

But it's too late. People appear at the edges of the arena, drawn by the commotion. More guards stream into the pit.

I have failed.

MIA

I'm half-asleep when the door is thrown open. Zake strides in, all smiles.

"Mia!" He squats down in front of me, speaking in a sing-song voice. "What news I have for you!" I sit up, and he untangles my rope. "Your ogre got caught trying to escape," he says merrily. My blood freezes in my veins. "He broke right through his cage. What did you tell him to upset him so much, little Mia, and turn him into a monster?"

I close my eyes. I'm out of options now.

What will they do to Cragnorr?

"Ah, yes," Zake says when I don't answer. "You *are* pregnant, aren't you?" He hoots. "Well, this has all worked out rather well for me." He tugs on my rope. "Are you ready for the surprise?"

I don't even want to imagine what he has in store for me—or for Cragnorr.

Zake tugs me along behind him as we depart the house that's

become my prison, and head toward the arena. People have already gathered there, and they're roaring and jeering.

"You didn't get started without me, did you?" the King calls out as he approaches his rickety wooden dais. Everyone cheers as we ascend the steps. It's sunset now, and the ground looks like it's covered in blood.

Down below, in the pit and all alone, is Cragnorr. He's strung up by his arms and legs to a set of posts that have been erected in the middle of the arena. A huge man dressed in all black stands nearby, with a long, curling whip in his hand.

Oh no. My Cragnorr.

"No!" I yank on my rope. "What are you going to do to him?" I shout the question, even though I already know the answer. There's only one thing that whip could mean.

"Twenty lashes. At least." Zake grins at me. "Why don't you take a seat and enjoy the show?"

Cragnorr gazes up at me, and when my eyes find his, he smiles a wan smile. He has a huge black eye, and bruises mottle his dark green body.

What have they done to him?

I have to stop this somehow. I can't watch my Cragnorr suffer, or my heart might just break in two.

"You don't have to do this," I tell the King, sitting down on the floor next to him the way he likes, his jewels and treasures piled high around us as if to remind him always how rich he is. "Cragnorr only tried to escape because of me. It's my fault. Please, don't blame him. Don't hurt him."

Zake tilts his head at me. "You're saying I should whip you, too?"

A cold shiver passes down my spine. I should've known better than to try to bargain, because he will take every possible opportunity to show he's smarter and meaner than I am.

He chuckles at my expression. "I can't risk it," he says. "Don't worry, you're safe as long as you're carrying that *thing* inside you." He turns back to the arena and raises his arms into the air, making the crowd go wild. "But your ogre isn't. He's done his job now. His purpose is served."

Served? Does that mean Zake is going to kill him?

A sob threatens to burst out of me, but I grit my teeth to hold it inside. I can't give him the gratification of my tears.

Down below, the big man in all black lifts the whip. Cragnorr watches me and only me, his amber eyes focused on my face. I want to look away as the whip flies back, but I can't. I have to be his lifeline. I have to witness his pain, as no one else will. I have to be his anchor.

The whip cracks as it lances the other direction in a perfect serpentine, and it feels like time has slowed. I can't look away from Cragnorr's face, the heavy, square jaw, the furrowed brows, his huge tusks and thick lips that are so perfect for kissing. I want to memorize him now before everything changes.

The sound of the whip splitting open flesh fills the air. Cragnorr's eyes go wide and his brow creases further, but he lets out no sound as the whip reels back again, now licked by blood. I cover my mouth, my hands trembling as the second blow lands across his back. Now Cragnorr's eyes squeeze shut as he tries not to cry out his agony.

I find myself whispering his name as a third blow lands. A ghost of each lash echoes in my own body, and I crumple to the ground as the crack of the whip can be heard around the arena. Blood drips down Cragnorr's body, splattering the ground.

There is an odd silence among the crowd, like they're transfixed by the bloodshed. These brutes, these cretins, leering at my ogre's suffering for their entertainment... I hope they are haunted forever.

By the fifth lash, Cragnorr's knees are shaking and his teeth are gritted. Blood is splashed across the floor of the arena, and I wonder if by the twentieth lash, he will simply bleed to death.

It isn't until the tenth lash that Cragnorr makes a sound: a moan of agony as his inflamed wounds are thrashed over and over again. I find his gaze, and there's a brutish determination in them. He won't let this crush him—but it might just crush me.

I can't watch him die. I will do anything if they would just stop.

"Please," I beg Zake, shaking his knee. "You can end this. He's learned his lesson. He's suffered enough." I swallow hard, my voice trembling. "Whip me, instead. I'll take his place. Just let him go!"

The King glares down at me as the whip snaps again, and agony races down my spine. Cragnorr's pain fills me up, and despite how hard I've tried to keep them at bay, tears pool in my eyes. It's almost unbearable for me—how can Cragnorr still be standing?

"You don't think he can handle it?" Zake says with a wicked grin. "You have so little faith in him."

Suddenly, he stands up and raises his arms into the air. Down below, the man in black pauses, letting the whip settle beside him.

"The ogre's woman begs for mercy," he calls out to the crowd, and they respond with jeers and boos. "What say you? Leniency? Or..." Zake turns to look at me and winks. "Perhaps thirty lashes instead of twenty?"

Roars and cheers rise up all around the arena. I clap my hand over my mouth, and my heart shatters. What have I done? Have I doomed him?

Cragnorr offers me a sad smile as I crumple to my knees. He doesn't blame me, but I will always blame myself. His blood will be on my hands forever.

Zake gives the order, and the man in black slings the whip back once more. The King sits down again, and even has the gall to yawn as another horrible *smack!* rings out.

This time, Cragnorr's legs finally give out, and he collapses in the arena. The ropes binding him keep his arms held above his head as blood streams down his thighs to the ground. His head bows forward, and I wonder if he's passed out from so much blood loss.

Another agonizing *crack* echoes around the pit. He's going to die out there. Zake is going to kill him in front of me, before he can even meet his child.

Where misery and remorse have occupied all of my soul, suddenly it is filled with a blinding rage. I can't let this man continue, not for a moment longer. The King is the scum of the earth, the true face of evil, and I can't bear his existence in this world. I cannot stand by and watch as he tortures my beloved ogre, inching him toward death.

Zake likes to keep his jewels near, even up here on the dais. He decorates with them, piling tables high with them, surrounded by his opulence. And among those jewels, I notice a golden point. It's buried underneath necklaces, rings, and coins, but the sharp tip reflects the hot sun.

I don't know what it is, but before I can think twice about it, I've taken advantage of my slack rope and snatched up the blade in my hand. It's a gold letter opener with a jeweled hilt, one that he probably didn't think twice about leaving out in the open. I have a single chance to do this, and I'd better make it count.

Zake only has time to glance down at me, confusion in his eyes, before I surge up to my feet with the long letter opener in hand. My vision is consumed with the sight of Cragnorr's blood, with the sound of his agonized cries. My body fills with my wrath, my guilt, and my unshakeable love for my silent ogre.

Gru and Narria are both too far away to stop me. In one swift movement, throwing all the strength I can behind it, I bury the letter opener in Zake's exposed throat.

Down below, I hear Cragnorr roar, but I'm too focused on driving the letter opener deeper and deeper, until the golden tip emerges from the other side of his neck, covered in blood. Gru and Narria are both frozen, staring in shock as I rip the letter opener back out again, showering myself with blood.

The entire arena goes silent. The lashes stop. All eyes are riveted on me.

Gru approaches us, his jaw hanging open. I position the letter opener in front of me, daring him to try to bring me down. I'll kill him, too, if I have to. I'll kill anyone who stands between Cragnorr and I.

On the other hand, Narria remains where she is, the slightest smile tugging up her lips. She crosses her arms, like none of this has surprised her.

It feels like minutes pass as no one moves, or even breathes. I'm panting, blood dripping down my front. I take no pleasure in death, but I will do anything to protect Cragnorr.

"Mia!" he calls out, his voice rough with his pain.

Then, all around me, the crowd begins to cheer.

CRAGNORR

What has she done?

I can take twenty lashes, even thirty. I could take a hundred if it meant protecting her. But I cannot protect Mia after this.

Blood spurts from the king's throat as she stumbles backward, clutching her weapon in hand. She's covered in red, soaking her front. I expect she'll be hanged for this, and my throat closes. I can't lose her and our budding whelp like this. I would rather die myself.

The King's closest guards advance on Mia while she readies herself to attack again.

"Mia!" I call out, finding my voice at last. I fight my chains, trying to get to my feet so I can get to her. I will throw my body in front of hers.

Then... everyone watching goes wild. The assembled people scream, hoot and howl, a pure eruption of noise. Mia stares down at them, as mystified as I am.

"Queen!" a woman in the crowd shouts. "Hail to the queen!"

The call catches fire. Others start echoing her. "Queen! Hail to the queen!"

Mia stands there, half of her face and her shoulder dripping blood, and slowly lowers her weapon. My own back is covered in blood, too, as if we are linked together by it.

The screaming grows in volume. "Queen! Queen!" Up on the King's dais, the tall woman with the braid approaches Mia. Too stunned by what's happening, Mia allows the other woman to grab her arm and raise it in the air. The crowd goes even more wild.

"We have a new queen!" shouts the braided woman.

Mia gazes out at the crowd, mystified, as they holler and scream. "Queen! Queen!"

At last, she seems to recover her senses. The woman whispers something to her, and Mia straightens her back, raising her other arm in the air, too.

"Silence!" But she can barely be heard over the cheers. "Shut the fuck up!" she roars at the top of her lungs, and the crowd abruptly quiets. Everyone stares up raptly at the dais, where Mia stands with the dead body of the King behind her.

"Release him at once!" she shouts, pointing down at me. "And bring him immediate medical attention!" The man in black stands frozen for a moment, before Mia stomps her foot and points. "Now!"

Then my binds are being untied, and I fall to the ground without them to hold me up. The searing pain in my back is worse than any I've ever felt, and my legs can't bear my weight. Four guards rush out, surrounding me, and I expect them to slap manacles on me—but instead they reach for my arms and lift me up, one on each side to help hold my weight. They lead me, hobbling, out of the arena and back into the holding area, where all the cages now sit empty.

Instead of being put inside one, I'm led up the steps, back the way I came when we were first captured. The guards guide me through the camp, to a lopsided tent where an elderly man is already holding the flap open.

"Here," he snaps, and I'm brought in to find a cot to one side. I don't fight as I'm laid upon it on my belly, my bloody, lacerated back exposed to the air.

"This is going to hurt, big guy," the healer says as he brings a cloth covered in fluid down to my wounds. "Just don't kill me, all right?"

It burns as it touches my raw wound, but I grit my teeth and bear it as he applies a topical treatment. The man in black had made a point of hitting the same places over and over to deepen the pain, and those hurt the most when the healer works on them.

But it doesn't matter. None of it matters. If these deranged people have made my woman their queen, and she is safe, I will be happy for the rest of my life.

MIA

I'm in a daze as Narria holds up my hand in the air. The people are chanting, "Queen! Queen!"

"What the fuck is happening?" I mutter, still baffled.

Narria leans over to bring her mouth to my ear. "You killed him," she says. "That makes you next in line."

What? By killing Zake... I've done this?

I wish I'd known *that* rule.

But they listened to me when I demanded they free Cragnorr, and he was led off without chains. I hope they do what I ask and get him help. No matter how his physical wounds heal, though, he may never truly recover from what's happened here today.

"Now say something inspiring," Narria says, shoving me to the front of the dais to overlook the crowd. "Be... queenly."

"But I'm not!" I have no idea what such a thing entails. I want nothing to do with what Zake created here, or these horrible people. "I'm not a queen."

"It doesn't matter!" Narria hisses. "You just murdered the king. You have to show strength, or they'll change their minds quick."

Fuck, she's right. I know they're capricious, as evidenced by every one of the fights I've witnessed in this pit.

I try to think of a speech. What do a bunch of lawless drunks want to hear?

"Well," I call out, trying to put as much confidence as I can into it, even if I feel like a mouse under a shoe. "You made a question-able decision today by choosing me."

The crowd is absolutely silent. Narria gives me a look like I'm a colossal idiot.

"But you made a questionable decision the day you chose him, too, so what's new?" I point at Zake's dead body, now propped in his fancy chair, head toppled forward and blood covering his front.

A few chuckles down below. Good. Okay. "I'm not what you want," I continue on. "I'm just a girl who ran away from home in her nightgown after cutting her neighbor's hand off."

More murmurs.

"I'm practically married to an ogre." I gesture down to the pit, where he was being whipped only minutes ago. "In fact, I'm pregnant. With his child."

More silence. Surely this is where this ends. I had a good opportunity here, one to save both my and my ogre's hides, and I'm ruining it.

Then a hoot goes up from the crowd. A few others join him. "The ogre-fucking queen!" someone shouts.

"The ogre-fucking queen!" It becomes the new chant, and quickly spreads through the crowd. Hands go up in the air, and people are soon screaming the words. "The ogre-fucking queen!"

I look over at Narria helplessly. I need some way out of this.

"The ogre-fucking queen, as she said, is very pregnant," Narria calls out, bringing down the chaos once more so they can hear her. "So she's going to get some rest, and then there will be a *marvelous* feast tonight, isn't that right?"

Right. "A truly wondrous feast!" I cry out. I've spent enough time sitting on the ground at Zake's side to know what to say. "We will celebrate a new era by rolling out the extra beer! All rounds on me!"

Narria helps me down the steps of the wooden platform while people scatter. My legs are shaking hard, my whole body alive with the terror, thrill, and relief.

Still, I manage to tell her firmly, "I need to see Cragnorr. Now."

CHAPTER 21

CRAGNORR

I've been set up on a cot, my body weight nearly crushing the thing, lying on my belly. My wounds have all been treated, the big ones stitched, and covered with poultices and bandages. Then the healer left me alone without even a guard posted at the door.

"Cragnorr?" a small voice says. I jerk to one side, which causes a terrible pain to ripple through my body.

It's Mia. My Mia.

I try to sit up, but she stops me with a hand on my shoulder. "No, no. Stay down. I'll sit with you." She kneels on the floor next to my bed, making sure to maintain contact between us. "I'm so sorry this happened. That I let them do that to you."

I give her a baffled look. She did nothing to cause this. I was the one who tried to escape. She stopped it by... well, murdering a king.

It was phenomenal, actually.

I take her hand in mine and bring it to my lips. She is incredible. A marvel of a woman, and I was given the greatest gift of all to be her mate.

"I should have killed that asshole a long time ago," Mia says, caressing my hand as she surveys the wounds on my back. "I'm so sorry, Cragnorr." She leans her head down next to mine and kisses the tip of my nose.

I shake my head. She shouldn't be sorry for anything. In response, I kiss her lips, and then scoot over on the tiny cot so she can lie next to me. Just moving makes my torn flesh scream, but I bear it to be closer to her.

"I don't know what all this 'queen' business is about," Mia huffs as she curls up next to me. "They're going to be sorely disappointed. Can I elect a different queen? Is that within my powers?"

I shrug and kiss her forehead. If they've really made her their next leader, then why not do whatever she likes?

"Yeah," she says, snapping her fingers. "That's what I'll do. I hope if I pick someone, though, they don't have to kill me first."

My hand instinctually tightens around hers, but she just laughs. "Don't worry. I won't let that happen." She's facing me as she draws my hand down her body to her soft abdomen. "Not while I have the two of you."

I close my eyes and simply hold her there, imagining a world where I can have my mate and my whelp both. I will show them the best life imaginable.

Soon someone arrives with food for me, and it's real food— *fresh* food. Even though I have to eat in a strange position, it's marvelous and life-changing to devour apples and cooked venison.

"Bathe him, too," Mia says to the guard as she gets off the cot, giving me one last peck on the cheek. "Sponge him down if you have to. He shouldn't be this dirty."

Without a second thought, the guard obeys her, leaving to fetch water.

Mia hovers by the door. I give her a curious look as I eat. "I would kill anyone for you," she says to me under her breath. "I'd kill him again if I had to. Ten times over."

I almost choke on the wave of emotion that threatens to wash me under. I have found the best woman in this whole complicated universe.

After blowing me one last kiss, she slips out of the room.

MIA

I wish I could say there was a lot involved in putting on a big feast, but really, Narria and Gru do everything. The little man is clearly peeved with how this has turned out, but he also seems afraid of me now.

"I'm not doing this," I tell Narria as I make my way to the head of the table, where Zake's elaborate, jewel-encrusted, tree trunk of a chair sits. I awkwardly stand next to it. "Can you bring me a regular chair?" I ask her. "Can I have your chair?"

Narria gives me an odd look as I drag away Zake's monstrosity and take hers instead. Everyone in the room is watching me, all while trying to pretend like they're carrying on their own conversations.

"You're not doing what?" Narria asks as she produces another chair to sit on.

"This 'queen' stuff, whatever it is." I look her over, contemplating the choice I'm about to make. She's decent as far as outlaws go, and people here respect her. She was the King's second in command, which should give her plenty of legitimacy.

"You have to do this 'queen' stuff," she hisses in my ear. "You killed him. You take the crown. Now you're queen, whether you like it or not, if you want to keep your own head, too."

I shudder. I know how easily the bandits can turn on someone.

"No," I say firmly. "I'm giving it to you. In exchange for the chair."

Narria scowls deeply. "You can't just hand it off to someone else!" she says in a hushed tone. "That's not how this works."

"Why not?" A big plate of freshly-barbecued ribs are set down in front of me, and I hastily grab one. My mouth is watering after the weeks spent tied up in Zake's house, awaiting whatever scraps he would spare for me. "I'm the queen. A queen can do whatever she wants, right?"

Narria's mouth works, but nothing comes out. Her frown deepens even further. "I guess so," she says uneasily.

"Well, there we are, then." I slap her on the back as I stand up. The tent quiets down, and people turn to me expectantly. "It's decided."

"Nothing is decided!"

I ignore her as I raise my empty mug in the air. "Thank you, everyone, for coming to eat with me," I call out across the assembled degenerates. "I hope you can understand why I won't join in the drinking tonight, though."

"The ogre-fucking queen!" somebody shouts, and a few others let out a *hurrah*!

"That's what I'd like to talk about. First, though, I have some decrees."

"Decrees?" Gru asks, brow furrowed.

"Orders? Requests." I shrug. "I can make those, can't I? It's in my power?"

"I suppose so," he says, uncertain. "His Majesty gave orders whenever he wanted."

"Wonderful." I take a deep breath, hoping I don't fuck up this massive opportunity I've been given. "Then here is my first decree: Cragnorr and I will be allowed to come and go as we please."

"*Go?*" whispers Narria, concern crossing her face. "You can't—"

"We will come and go as we please!" I shout, my voice strong and firm. Narria's eyes go wide, then she hastily sits back down in her chair. Some people are murmuring, so I quickly follow it up with, "Shut up!"

They listen, and silence falls again.

"For my second decree..." I turn to Narria. "I am giving away the title of queen."

The tent erupts in furious noise.

"She can't do that!" someone cries.

"That's not how it works!"

Sighing, I climb up onto the chair, and then onto the table. I stomp my foot a few times on the hard wood to get everyone's attention, and once again they fall quiet.

"Why not?" I demand. "I am queen. I can do whatever the fuck I want!" I reach down and take Narria's hand. "Get up here," I whisper to her.

Very annoyed, she does what I ask and gets onto the table with me.

"Now..." I begin, studying her. "This one will make a fine queen, won't she?"

Confusion ripples out across the crowd. A few people hit their tables with mugs.

"Yes!" I hold Narria's arm up into the air. "I have decided! This is your new queen now!"

There are some hoots and hollers, and a lot of arguing. People can't seem to agree on whether I can do what I'm doing or not.

"But the ogre-fucking queen's not dead!" a woman shouts. "She has to be dead!"

"Who says?" I snap back.

Narria stomps her foot on the table. "Listen, you fucking warts!" she shouts. "The queen said it's so, so that means it's so!"

Clearly, she was the right choice for the job, because she's only met by a few irritated grumbles.

When the dust has settled and the celebrating has resumed, Narria glares at me.

"I can't believe you saddled me with this," she growls. "After everything I've done for you."

I shrug. "Sorry."

She shakes her head. "You've been a pest since the beginning. As if that would change anytime soon." Her gaze darkens. "You're going to leave, aren't you?"

I nod slowly. "We can't stay."

Narria lets out a defeated sigh. "Fine. Get the fuck out of here. See if I miss you." Then her lip quirks up at the side.

That night, an additional bed is brought into the tent where Cragnorr is recovering, and I sleep beside him, our hands linked. The healer attends to his wounds again in the morning, but it will be a slow process of healing. Only once he's on his feet again can we finally leave this place behind us.

Though it seems my transfer of power was successful, and Narria has taken up residence in Zake's old lopsided house, a few people still mutter "the ogre-fucking queen" when they walk by. Some even nod in respect, though I'm nobody special now.

Then, at last, after weeks of his skin stitching itself back together, Cragnorr is able to move properly without pain. I've never been so relieved to see him up and walking around again that I jump onto him, throwing my arms around his neck and my legs around his waist. He hums with pleasure, cradling me against him as he kisses my throat.

Let's just say that the healer makes a point of not returning that night as our cries echo around the camp.

What a joy it is, to be reunited with my ogre, the thrumming center of my heart.

CRAGNORR

At long last, it is time to leave this hellish place behind. I walk away utterly changed, from my fresh scars to my full heart.

Narria, the fearsome woman with the braid, orders people around until a wagon is filled up with goods. We have food, drink, building supplies, basic tools, firewood, and clothing. None of it fits me, of course, but we will remedy that when we find our new home.

Where that will be, of course, is a mystery to us yet.

We're also gifted a horse to pull our new wagon: an irritable brown mare who only seems to like Mia. As we reach the gates to the town, she slips the horse another apple, and I can't imagine why it prefers her.

We don't want to attract a crowd, so the gates are opened discreetly. I decide not to ride the horse, as large as I am, but I do lift up Mia and set her on top so she doesn't have to walk. I think often of our whelp growing in her belly, and I want to protect her from all the discomforts this world might try to inflict.

Mia waves goodbye to Narria, who gives an irritated flick of her wrist in return. She may pretend she doesn't like us, but I can tell she has a soft spot for my sweet woman, like most everyone does.

Then we're off, down the path we once traveled together and stumbled upon a net. We walk for a few miles in quiet, until suddenly Mia says, "Do you know where we're going?"

I pause and glance up at her, perplexed. I thought she knew where we were headed.

A bright laugh falls from her lips. "You don't know either, huh?" She brings our horse to a stop, and peers around the woods. "I guess we could go anywhere. But we should probably stay far from any human towns—and trollkin ones, too."

I nod in agreement. Her kind are a danger to me, and mine are a danger to her. Together we're strange and unusual, and it will be difficult for us to find a safe home in a world that will inevitably have a problem with us.

"Hmm." Mia leans back, thinking. "I suppose... we should just keep looking until we find the right place. Somewhere we want to raise our kid." She grins and pats her belly. "Peaceful. Quiet." Then her expression falls. "But I don't want to be alone, Cragnorr."

But there's nowhere we could go that we won't be alone. It's a necessity if we want to live the peaceful life she wants.

"Wait a second!" Mia sits up abruptly on the horse's back. "There was this guy, the one who told Zake that humans and trollkin could have babies together. He said he found out in Eyra Cove. It's one of the neutral cities." She looks puzzled for a moment. "I have no idea how we would reach it, but clearly others like us are living there. It's a neutral city, and if we can just figure out..." Mia trails off, now lost in thought. I wait patiently while she ponders the question of how we cross an ocean together. I certainly don't know how, but if anyone can find us a path to our destination, it's her.

"We split up."

My heart catches in my throat when she says it. I reach for her hand and seize it in mine, shaking my head fervently. She gives me a pitying look. "I know, I know. But it would only be temporary. I can't take you on a human ship, and you can't take me on a trollkin ship. If we could just get there, though..." She leans down and takes my cheeks in her hands, so I have to look right into her big, brown eyes. "Then we can be together forever."

Though everything in me riots at the idea of being apart from Mia, I know she's right. I swallow hard.

"A cave?" I finally venture, and she jolts up at the sound of my voice.

"I would love to live in a cave with you," she says, straightening on the bored mare's back. "But what happens when the baby comes? What if something goes wrong?" She shakes her head. "I know it seems dangerous, but we can do it. I know we can. And then we'll be safe, at last."

This warning strikes me deep in the belly. She's right. How often have ogres and humans created offspring? Rarely, I would imagine. It might be best to do as she says and find this city of hers, as much as it pains me to think of parting with her—not when we have done everything we can to be together again.

My heart almost can't bear the idea, but Mia looks so resolute, I am forced to agree with her.

"Good," she says, patting my head when she sees I've finally given in. "Then we'll stop by Sackett, pick up a map, and make our plan from there. All right?"

I nod, and she smiles brightly at me.

"Don't worry," she says as we begin walking again. "We'll always find our way back to each other."

And I know that she's right. Nothing will keep us apart, not ever again.

CHAPTER 22

MIA

I am not impressed by the map.

It shows mostly human cities, with vague symbols for trollkin-occupied areas. We sit around the fire as the sun sets, poring over it together, trying to find the best path possible for each of us.

I worry about Cragnorr traveling alone, as unusual as ogres are, even among trollkin kind. It's not like I've ever traveled by sea before, either. I give him the map so he can point out his destination to whoever he asks along the way, but before I can let it go, he pulls me into his lap, ensconcing me in his arms. I feel him trembling as we talk about parting ways.

"It will be all right, I promise," I tell him, caressing his cheek, then running my finger down his long tusk. "And then we'll have the life we've always dreamed about."

He nods in understanding, but doesn't seem any happier about it. That night, he pushes me down to my bedroll and lavishes attention on me, kissing every part of my body, wringing the pleasure out of me, savoring me as long as he can, like he's saving it all up for the weeks we'll be separated.

Then we meet the fork in the path where we will each go our own way. He'll walk, and I'll take the horse, which I'll sell before getting on the boat. We won't need it where we're going. We split the coin that Narria sent with us two ways, but before I can set foot going the other direction, Cragnorr wraps me up in his embrace.

"I know," I whisper to him. His hand travels around my middle, and he grows tense all over. "It will be some time before the baby is here. I'll be fine. I promise."

After a few charged moments, he puts me back down again, and his soft eyes are red. With one last kiss, we set off on our journeys, and I hope that he makes it without me.

It's a long, boring ride to the nearest port city, taking me over rolling hills, broad valleys, and through increasingly bigger and bigger towns. Every night as I camp with the horse, who I've affectionately named Apple, I think about Cragnorr and where he is now. Has he reached the trollkin port city yet? Is he eating? Has he been accosted?

But I know I can't dwell on it. I just have to hope this hasn't all been for nothing, and we'll see each other again on the other side.

At last, the bright aquamarine ocean appears on the horizon, and I could almost fall over with my relief. I'm that much closer to being reunited with my ogre again.

I'm able to sell Apple, the wagon and our supplies in the port city for a good chunk of change, which should help us get started in Eyra Cove. I don't know much about it besides the fact it's on an island, part of an archipelago far out in the ocean. I've never even seen the sea before, and now I'm about to get onto a ship and travel far out into the nothingness, hoping I won't wash away.

At last, I'm on board the great ocean liner headed for the Frattern Islands, and I retreat quickly into the cabin of the ship because the sight of unending water has made me a little sick to my stomach.

I don't know if it's the rocking of the boat or the baby growing inside me, but I have to hurl over the side at least four or five times a day as we make our way. A man on board tries to hit on me while I stand at the railing, my face green, so I promptly throw up on him.

No one else approaches me the rest of the voyage.

I'm awoken by a horn blowing. Grabbing my money pouch, I rush up to the deck to find out what's going on.

When I emerge from below deck, I find great, tall cliffs ahead of us. For a moment I'm certain that the captain is about to wreck the ship, when I notice there's a city nestled among them.

At last. I've made it.

I'm the first one off the ship when we arrive, and everyone recognizes me as the puking lady, so they let me go. Once I'm on solid ground again, I could simply kiss it.

The city is abuzz with life as people bustle from one place to the next. There are humans and trollkin alike here, all stopping at the same storefronts and stumbling drunkenly out of the same bars. It's like nothing I've ever seen before.

I didn't see Cragnorr at the dock, so either he's already here and went to get lunch, or he hasn't made it yet. I wring my hands, hoping he won't be too long yet—and that nothing has happened to him on his way.

We agreed to wait for each other at the dock, but I'm desperate to eat real food again, so I pick my way through the crowds toward an inn. After stuffing my empty stomach full, I head back to where a dozen ship masts bob on the water to begin my wait for Cragnorr. It could be hours or days, but regardless, I'll stand here until he arrives from sun up to sun down. We won't have a home yet, but I can sleep at the inn.

On the way, though, a little blue trollkin boy goes racing past me, nearly sweeping my legs out from under me.

"Sorry, lady," he says in Freysian, ducking his head remorsefully. "You okay?"

I stare at him. "I'm fine, thank you." To get a better look, I crouch down. "How do you speak my language?"

He quirks an eyebrow like I'm an idiot.

"Well, my mom's human," he says. "And look around you." I follow his finger to the wide variety of humans and trollkin alike passing by us.

That makes sense. One probably needs to speak both languages to live here.

But wait. Did I really hear him right?

"Your mom's a human, you said?" I ask eagerly.

He squints at me, trying to suss me out. Finally he answers, "Yeah, did you not hear me the first time?"

"Can I meet her?"

It looks like the boy might run away, but after studying me a moment longer, he sighs in annoyance.

"Okay, fine. Follow me."

The boy leads me across a gangway, over rocky cliffs toward the mercantile end of town. It isn't long weaving through other citygoers before he stops in front of a shop, and peers over the counter.

"Mom!" he calls out. A head of bright red hair appears in the back, and a woman with pale, freckled skin emerges from behind a stack of furs. She smiles brightly.

"Izzek! You're early."

"Yeah," he grumbles. "This lady wanted to meet you."

The woman quirks an eyebrow at me, and I rub the back of my head. Without further ado, the boy takes off running again, vanishing into the crowd.

"How can I help you?" the woman asks, curiosity gleaming in her green eyes.

"Well, um... your son is... trollkin, right?" I gesture at where he was standing moments before.

She nods, and her face echoes her son's suspicion. "He's a troll, yes," she answers carefully.

I wave my hands to show I come in peace. "Well, you see, I..." Where do I even begin? "I'm pregnant." I gesture at my belly, and the woman's eyebrows rise. "And the father is an, um, an ogre."

Her surprise transforms into a huge, white smile.

"You don't say!" She claps her hands. "An ogre! I thought they were all gone."

I shake my head. "Nope. I have one of my very own."

"Well, where is he?" She glances around us meaningfully. "He's safe here."

"That's why we came." I hold out one hand. "My name is Mia. And I'm hoping you can help me."

CRAGNORR

It is a long and dreary trip to the town on the coast, and then across the sea, filled with wide-eyed stares. Neither trolls nor orcs are sure what to make of an ogre in their midst, but none try to stop me or accost me. I don't know if it's my size or my reputation, but I'm glad to be left alone.

The ocean is beautiful, but I can also tell by the vastness of it that it's dangerous. I keep to my cabin and patiently wait, thinking only of my Mia's soft body and warm eyes, until at last, we reach our destination.

I'm nearly out of money, given how much I need to eat, so I'll have to find work if I don't come across Mia immediately. If she's not there waiting for me... I just have to hope nothing has happened to her.

All my worries are wiped away when I spot a woman standing on the dock with flowing black hair in even longer waves than I remember. She wears a lightweight shirt that does not obscure the swell of her belly, and my relief nearly overwhelms me.

"Mia," I say, and she spins around at the sound of my voice. A huge smile sweeps across her face, and she doesn't waste a moment charging towards me. She leaps into my arms and I swing her into the air, twirling her around me and reveling in the sound of her sweet, wild laughter.

"Cragnorr," she murmurs, stroking my hair and nuzzling her cheek against mine. "You made it."

All I can do is hug her closer, showing her with my body how at last, everything is how it should be, now that we're together again.

As I expected, my Mia has been up to quite a lot while she was waiting for me.

She's found us a home—a very odd one tucked into a back corner of the city, constructed against the cliffs. It's rather separate from the other houses, isolated high up where no one else was brave enough to build, which will suit me, I think. It is the cave of houses.

Mia knows me well.

It is decrepit, though, and will require many repairs to be livable for my woman and our whelp. I am fully up to the task of fixing it.

My gregarious Mia has also made us some new friends: another human-trollkin couple, who already have a child of their own.

"I hear yours was much easier to make," the woman says, winking at me. "We've been trying for another, but no luck yet."

Their son, a blue troll with a wild mane of red hair, covers his ears and sings *la la la*. His father snorts, and I am pleased that Mia has already found community here, which I know she craves.

Then, at last, we are alone. We will sleep on the floor until I can build us a bed, and Mia has already found work so she can pay for the wood. She is using her father's jewelry-making skills to apprentice for a silversmith, and it will be enough to support us until I can also put myself to good use.

But first, the bed, so I can at last have a comfortable place to enjoy my mate.

CHAPTER 23

MIA

We've already started decorating, even as the roof is being repaired to properly keep out the rain. Cragnorr has built a massive bed for the two of us, and that's what I'm most looking forward to using. He's found work down on the dock, loading and unloading ships, and he's so good at it—and can move so much cargo—that they pay him time-and-a-half.

After weeks of making our home livable in between shifts, we start up the fire pit, and we choke ourselves on smoke until we remember to open the flue. The sounds of the city are far off, just a faint murmur in the distance. We have already settled in well here, in this unusual place with its frigid winds, seagull cries, and salty sea air.

After we've cooked on our new stove and eaten our fill, Cragnorr picks me up and carries me off to our bedroom without a word, as is his style.

Together we lie on our new bed, reveling in it. Cragnorr scoots down so he can press his face to my belly, where he kisses it all over. He already started building the cradle in the other room.

He travels up my body with his lips, over the fabric of my tunic, until he reaches my mouth. There, he pauses, and draws some hair back from my face.

"My Mia," he says quietly, bracketing my cheeks with his big tusks. He palms my whole hand, cocooning it there. He's thick and hard against my thigh, but tonight he seems like he wants to take his time.

And I'll let him, because we have all the time in the world.

CRAGNORR

I will worship my woman until I'm old and wrinkled. Perhaps I knew from the moment she found me in that tree that we were meant to be. Mia is my shining star, my light in the darkness, the gold among the silver and bronze. She is the heart of my world.

Whenever I think of my whelp growing inside her, I grow hungry—ravenous. The taste of her cunt has changed in a delightful way, and she is even more needy now, asking for my cock every night and sometimes in the morning, too.

I will happily give it to her forever.

She mewls as I slowly take her mouth in mine, savoring the softness of her lips, the luscious caress of her tongue. Just kissing her this way is the balm I need. When we're together, everything else disappears except her warm body next to mine.

I plan to make good use of our new bed, though, so I trail my lips down her jaw, over her ear, where I breathe gently against it. She shivers all over, wiggling her way even closer to me, her hips pressing against mine.

She wants me, and that feeling is still the most intoxicating of all.

Her breasts are growing bigger and heavier as her belly swells, but they're also more sensitive now, so once I've taken off her tunic and thin undershirt, I wrap my lips around the nipples gently and suck as if I were a whelp myself. She moans and arches her back, so I give her more, and more, until I can't restrain myself any longer.

I scoot down the bed and roughly seize her legs in my hands. Once her pants are gone and she's panting underneath me in anticipation, I sling her legs over my shoulders and dive into her sweet cunt.

Oh, the taste of her is like nothing else. She moans sweetly as I lap her up, taunting her sensitive pearl until her small slit is shiny and her lower lips are swollen up. I wonder sometimes how my whelp will possibly fit through this, but she can take my cock, so her body must know how.

"Please," Mia begs, arching into my mouth after I've nursed her to her first climax. "Please, Cragnorr."

I can't deny her anything. I take off my trousers and her eyes get wide when I'm naked in front of her, the way they always do. Before I can kneel on the bed, she has me in her hands, those slim fingers wrapped around my cock, and that soft, wet tongue tantalizing the head. She licks up my dribble of seed, letting out hums of pleasure as she works it deeper into her mouth. My Mia loves to take me this way, grabbing my balls in one hand and stroking the root of me with the other. If I'm not careful, I'll go off in her mouth.

Though that doesn't usually stop my cock from waking up again when it's time to slide inside her. It always wants to fill her up with my seed, as if it doesn't know she's already full of me.

"Mia," I say quietly, earning a surprised look. I lift her chin, and my cock pulls free of her wet mouth with a *pop!* Gently I press her down to the bed, and she gets a mischievous look in her eyes as she obediently spreads her legs.

"Fuck me," she whispers as she touches herself in front of me. I love how even as she grows my whelp, sometimes she wants it rough, like the first time I took her. It stirs a heat low in my belly, and my vision narrows down to nothing but her. Red tinges the edges of the world, and that heat spreads across my body, driving me towards her.

I drag her to the edge of the bed so her slick cunt is at the perfect height for me, then position my cock between her soft folds.

"Please," she begs. She wants me. She *needs* me. It turns my blood hot, and with a roar, I thrust in.

Mia moans as I fill her completely in one motion. I find my place, deep inside her, right where I was always meant to be. Her sweet channel can't take all of me yet, but the longer I fuck her, the more it will open for me and welcome me, so I'd better get going.

I grip her thighs in my big hands, squeezing her soft flesh as I sink myself into her, watching as her tiny cunt swallows as much of me as it can. Rarely can she ever take more than two-thirds of me. It'll be hard to keep myself in check this time, watching her heavy breasts bouncing even more than before, her rounded belly rocking with every one of my strokes, here in our bed. *Our* bed, in *our* house, where we'll raise *our* whelp.

As Mia cries out beneath me, more and more of my cock vanishes into her, her sweet lips spread impossibly wide for me. She is beautiful, my mate. The most perfect being to ever live. I will make her mine, again and again, for the rest of time.

Mia

The way my ogre fucks me, it's like he is possessed. His eyes are narrowed, his pupils huge and black, his teeth gritted as if I am the sole focus of his attention. I feel like I'm at the center of his world, and he's the center of mine.

He rubs a hand down my belly as he thrusts inside me, those powerful hips slamming into me over and over. A growl falls from his lips as he cups it, smoothing over the swell that will eventually become our child. It's driven him a little wild, and I don't mind it in the least. Sometimes this madness comes over him, like it did when he killed the liger to protect me and then he took me roughly in the darkness. This is the hidden version of Cragnorr, the monster that's usually locked up inside him. It pleases me that I draw it out of him, that I can turn him into this animal who wants nothing more than to take ownership of me.

"Who do I belong to?" I ask as he plunders me, staking his claim. A visceral heat spreads across me with every stroke.

Cragnorr answers with a snarl. "Me. You are *mine.*"

He wraps his arms around my ass and hauls me up into his arms, guiding my hips up and down. I cling to his neck as he ravages me, pushing me against the slanted wall of our house to fuck me even harder. Heavy grunts punctuate my cries, and the stroke of his cockhead over my inner walls is sending sparks of pleasure swirling up my spine. My head falls back on the wall as my muscles tighten all over, and Cragnorr groans, his tusks tangling in my hair.

Nothing could compare to being with my ogre. His soul is as gentle and soft as his rage is wild. He is my tender, fierce animal, who cups my heart in his hand and treasures it.

The slap of our bodies meeting, the wet sound of him slicking in and out of me, is sending me spiraling higher and higher until my head is up in the clouds and I'm screaming out Cragnorr's name. I feel as if I could fly with him.

I am a wire strung as taut as possible, squeezing every part of my ogre. He moans as he stuffs that massive cock inside me over and over, and soon I can feel him swelling up, stretching my edges even wider.

My peak steals my voice. I convulse, and feel as if I might simply come disconnected from reality. Cragnorr buries himself deep, and his teeth clench the flesh of my shoulder as he explodes.

He stumbles back to the bed with me still speared on his cock, clutching me in his lap, while I shiver from the force of my finish. Cradling me tight, he kisses the top of my head.

"Thank you," he murmurs. "My Mia."

I get thick and round over the next few months. As we head into winter, Cragnorr and I spend more time in our bed. We learn all the complexities of each other's bodies. After a tip from my new friend, I find myself entertained by wrapping my lips around his cock and burying a few fingers in his tight ass. He does the same for me when we discover how good it feels, and it is marvelous, all the places he fits inside me.

Spring is coming again when I reach the point where I can no longer stay on my feet. I'm much too big, and the local healer visits every day to check on me. I'm given small doses of a green substance to keep the pain at bay, and I lie there for weeks, bored out of my skull. Cragnorr brings me books to read, but often simply lies down with me and holds me in the quiet.

"I can't wait to get rid of this baby," I tell him one evening, and as if on cue, she arrives.

CRAGNORR

I don't think I have ever felt worse than I do watching my mate in pain. It's far worse than the lashes, and I clutch her hand tight in mine as she cries and sobs her fury. It goes on all night, and soon she's running out of energy. I wipe her sweat away, and the healer assures us it will all be fine as long as she can push.

But as Mia's energy fades, I cling tighter to her. I wonder if I should never have learned about the cocks-in-cunts business. I don't like seeing her this way, not a bit.

"Fight," I whisper to her, both her hands clenched around my fingers. She nods and renews her fierce battle to give our whelp life.

And then, she lets out a wordless scream, and the healer sucks in a breath.

"An ogre?" the orc woman asks as Mia collapses, boneless, to the bed. She laughs as she brings our daughter over to us.

She does look much like me, without the tusks, of course. She'll grow those in as I did. Her face is so small, her nose and eyes so perfect, I almost can't bear to look at her.

"Give her here," Mia says in a mouse voice.

The healer leaves us, and we lie side by side on our big bed, our whelp latched onto my mate's rather big breasts. I'm already eager to sow another one in her, until our house is full of them.

We name our whelp after Mia's mother, who my poor mate will never see again. Marenna, who has dark grey-green skin, and big yellow eyes like mine, gets bigger rather quickly. It's not long before Mia can't even pick her up.

Marenna is a happy, burbling baby who loves to be carried in the crook of my arm around the city, and cries like a bullhorn when she's hungry. I love her like I've never loved another being, save for her mother.

One night, after our friends and their wild son have gone, I curl up with my Mia in bed while Marenna sleeps in her crib in the next room. I curl my arms around my mate and squeeze her breasts, rolling her nipples in my fingers. I make love to her slowly, earning many sobs of pleasure and even more silent screams. The happily-mated troll, Raz'jin, suggested that if I wanted to put another whelp in Mia, I ought to make her finish and "cream on my cock" as many times as possible before filling her.

"That'll make it stick," he'd said with a wink. His own mate, Telise, jabbed him with her elbow.

And so, once my Mia is twitching underneath me, her cunt perilously tight and soft around me, I finally release. I give her so much of my seed that it spills out everywhere, and so of course, I pull out my wet cock, and pump it until it's ready to fuck all my spend back into her again.

I'm not satisfied, of course, until my mate is swollen up with me once more—and even then, I know my body will never tire of hers, not as long as I'm alive. I wonder if our next one will come out human or ogre. I think Marenna will make a wonderful older sister.

I fall asleep every night with my human right where she belongs. The one who saved me, many times over.

She is mine. My Mia. My entire world.

THANK YOU SO MUCH FOR READING!

If you enjoyed this book, please consider leaving a review! Reviews are incredibly helpful to indie authors like me in reaching new readers.

You can also support me by buying my other books!

MORE FUN THINGS TO READ

Want to read Telise and Raz'jin's story? *Stealing the Troll's Heart* is the first book in my Trollkin Lovers fantasy series, where humans and trollkin are at war—but some may cross the lines for love.

Bred by the Wolfman follows a wolfman who only wants a cub of his own, and the anonymous surrogate who he realizes too late is his mate. It is the first in the *DreamTogether Breeding Program* series.

My Minotaur Husband is a sweet, fluffy, super steamy book about a human woman and her trial marriage to a rather... large minotaur.

Join My Newsletter!

For all the latest regarding books, and to get a FREE Trollkin Lovers novella, join my newsletter! You can also get paperback copies of your favorite books with artwork and stickers.

www.LyonneRiley.com

Also by Lyonne Riley

Trollkin Lovers

Stealing the Troll's Heart

Healing the Orc's Heart

Capturing the Orc's Heart

Charming the Troll's Heart

Keeping the Human's Heart

Finding the Troll's Heart

Tempting the Ogre's Heart

Enchanting the Ogre's Heart

Winning the Orc's Heart

DreamTogether Breeding Program

Bred by the Wolfman

Bred by the Dragon

Anthologies

The Monster Menagerie

Other Books

Seduced by the Werewolves

Five Gifts for the Blacksmith's Wife

Prince of Beasts

My Minotaur Husband

Programmed for Love

My Minotaur Husband

Programmed for Love

About the Author

I come from a traditional publishing background, which is rewarding but often too rigid, so I shifted to self-publishing to pursue my real passion in writing: extremely sexy monster romance. I probably should have known I would end up here after spending most of my young adulthood writing erotic fan fiction, but it took me a while to find my way back to myself.

Acknowledgments

I would like to thank everyone involved in helping me through the process of putting out this book. I can't say enough how much I appreciate the help and encouragement of the people around me—especially Amber, who told me I could do this in the first place.

Huge thank you to Ash Raven for the cover design. To my critique partners, Jenn, Ruth, Kassie, and Cia, who gave me phenomenal editorial feedback: You all make this possible. And of course, my amazing spouse, who has always supported my dreams—and given me lots of inspiration for my characters' sexy adventures.

I couldn't have done this without the expertise of my fellow self-published romance authors. Thank you for inviting me into your circles and helping me through this process.

And thank you to my readers, who gave this book a shot.